EMMA

AND THE

CIVIL WARRIOR

CANDY DAHL

Candy Dahl

CAROLINA MOON
PUBLISHING COMPANY

EMMA AND THE CIVIL WARRIOR
Published by Carolina Moon Publishing Company
P.O. Box 99622, Raleigh, NC 27624
(919) 848-9144
Copyright © 2001 by Candy Dahl

Printed in the United States of America
First Edition

Publisher's Cataloging-in-Publication
(Provided by Quality Books, Inc.)

Dahl, Candy.
Emma and the civil warrior / Candy Dahl. — 1st ed.
p. cm.
SUMMARY: In 1865 twelve-year-old Emma Graham strives
to help defeat the Union army in Raleigh, North Carolina,
through various acts of smuggling, spying, and stealing. After
Lieutenant George Round, General Sherman's signal officer,
befriends the Graham family, Emma struggles to accept the
truths that the end of the war brings.
Audience: Ages 8-12.
LCCN 00-110636
ISBN 0-9706358-3-4 (hardcover)
ISBN 0-9706358-4-2 (paperback)
1. North Carolina—History—Civil War, 1861-1865—
Juvenile fiction. 2. United States—History—Civil War, 1861-
1865—Juvenile fiction. 3. Sherman's March through the Caro-
linas—Juvenile fiction. I. Title.

PZ7.D15115Emm2001   [Fic]
                       QBI00-901939

10 9 8 7 6 5 4 3 2

For David, Matt, and Emily—
my three essentials.

And for the students in
Donna Craven's 1996-1997 Language Arts Class,
Lead Mine Elementary School,
Raleigh, North Carolina—
thanks for your encouragement
and for Micah.

ACKNOWLEDGMENTS

I consider myself to be fortunate—I know some really nice, intelligent, talented people. And I take this opportunity to express my thanks to them for the roles they have played in making this book possible:

To the North Carolina State Capitol Historian, Raymond Beck, who has unselfishly, and with great enthusiasm, shared his resources, his vast knowledge, and insider tours with me.

To my many writer friends for the bolstering that we do for one another, especially to the Triangle Circle Writers Group, to Eileen Heyes (copy editor extraordinaire), to Donna Sink (a person's best cheerleader), and to Stephanie Greene (editorial guru).

To teachers Donna Craven, Caryn Messinger, and Molly Molnar who have welcomed me into their classrooms to talk about characters and themes and vivid verbs and revision—to talk about writing.

And to all those attentive students who read, listened, interpreted, critiqued, and, ultimately, inspired me. We had fun, didn't we!

CHAPTER ONE

Tuesday, April 11, 1865

"Hide under here!" Aunt Lily pushed Emma toward Micah's bed, where he lay feverish and afraid.

"No." Emma stiffened and grabbed her aunt's arms. "You might need my help."

"Emma Graham, I will not sacrifice a twelve-year-old girl to the Yankees. Now get under that bed. And don't forget Molly."

Emma dropped to the floor and scooted into hiding. Her legs tangled in her skirt. She clutched her doll, Molly, in her arms. She could hear boots stomping on the plank floors below. Doors banged open. A gruff voice shouted, "What you call the 'bummers' is here!" Then laughter.

Emma prayed those Yankee bummers wouldn't climb the stairs, but before her "Amen" the bedroom door burst open. Aunt Lily gasped, but her dainty feet didn't move.

"What is the meaning of breaking into my home?" she asked.

"Sherman's men don't knock, Rebel woman." The man sounded like a growling dog. "We take what we want from Southern traitors."

Aunt Lily's feet tripped over one another as the man pushed past her. He bent low in a slow, mocking bow. Emma saw the black half-moons under his fingernails when his hand swept the ground.

"Guns and jewelry," he said. "Where are they?"

"I have none of those," Aunt Lily replied.

"We'll find them," he said, and his boots walked straight toward Micah's bed.

"Don't move the boy," Aunt Lily pleaded. "He's sick."

Suddenly Micah, Emma's five-year-old brother, was plopped down onto the floor. He turned his head and stared under the bed. Tears leaked from his eyes. Emma heard ripping sounds and watched as snow-white feathers floated down over Micah and caught in his red hair. But she knew there was no treasure hidden in the bed pillows.

When the mattress above her was jerked from the bed, light spilled over Emma. The man smirked and leaned close to stare into her face.

"What have we here?"

Emma gazed into the bloodshot eyes and smelled the unwashed body of a demon Yankee. His grimy hand shot toward her like a rattlesnake.

"No!" she screamed, shoving Molly behind her back.

From downstairs another man shouted.

"Charlie. We found the booty in the piano."

"I shoulda known to look there. Can't you dumb North Carolina Rebs come up with any original hidey-holes?" Charlie sneered at Aunt Lily as he rushed from the room.

"Stay here with Micah," Aunt Lily said in a shaky voice. She left and closed the bedroom door behind her.

Emma pulled herself out from under the bed. She knelt beside Micah and began picking feathers from his hair. Suddenly he sat up, and his skinny arms clutched her neck.

"Are those Yankees gonna kill us?" he whispered into her ear. "Are they killing Aunt Lily?"

Emma jumped to her feet, pulling Micah up with her. Taking his hand, she opened the door, and the two children tiptoed down the hall to Aunt Lily's bedroom. Emma lifted the fabric skirt of a dressing table.

"Squat down under here," she told Micah.

"Emma, don't leave me." He was still crying.

"You'll be safe here if you stay quiet. I must help Aunt Lily."

Micah crawled under the dressing table, pulled his legs up against his chest, and clasped his arms tightly around them. Emma reached behind him and dropped her doll to the floor.

"Keep Molly with you," she said as she stood and straightened the table skirt. The hem of it touched the floor, and her brother disappeared from sight.

"Shhh," she reminded him.

Emma crept downstairs, her back against the wall to avoid the creaks in the middle of each step. Inching down the hallway and peeking around the door of the parlor, she saw Aunt Lily standing ramrod straight just inside the room.

That smelly Charlie clutched fistfuls of jewelry and handguns. An old Sunday hat of Uncle James's sat cockeyed on his head.

"This is what we came for, fat woman," Charlie shouted into Aunt Lily's face. Specks of his spit glistened on her skin. Emma's stomach lurched at the sight.

Another Yankee shook a sack of flour over the parlor floor. A third one opened a jar, upended it, and poured black, sticky molasses over the white flour.

"Hope you like the supper we fixed you," Charlie said. "It's all you got."

With that, they suddenly left, galloping away on their horses.

As if in a daze, Aunt Lily walked slowly past smashed furniture and broken dishes onto her front porch. Emma followed, stood beside her, and held her ice-cold hand. Outside, the Yankees had torn down fences and killed two oxen. Aunt Lily and Uncle James's farm was in shambles.

They stood silent for a long time. When Aunt Lily chuckled, Emma jumped as if a gun had fired.

"They called me fat."

Emma stared at her aunt's face. The half smile disappeared and Aunt Lily's bottom lip quivered as if she were having a chill.

"Oh, Emma. The fields were greening with new wheat and early vegetables. Now it's all just trampled mud."

"But we fooled them, Aunt Lily," Emma said, trying to cheer her.

"Yes, we did, Emma, thanks to you. How did you know they'd check the piano?"

"Before Papa left for the war, Mother hid our silver in the piano. Papa laughed and said that was the first place a thief would look."

"I'm glad that memory stayed with you for

these three long years. Sure enough, those Yankees thought they were opening a treasure chest when they looked inside my piano."

The weak smile returned to Aunt Lily's face.

"Cheap jewelry and busted guns. That's all they got out of my hidey-hole."

Tucking dark curls into the bun at the base of her neck, Aunt Lily gazed at Emma with her green eyes.

"Not only do you look like me, my dearest niece, but I believe you've inherited my resourcefulness."

"Will they be back when they discover our trick?" Emma spoke around the lump of fear that she couldn't swallow.

"I don't think so."

Emma's stomach clenched with fright. She wanted Aunt Lily to *know* the Yankees wouldn't return.

Emma didn't understand this war at all. Why did the Yankees come to Aunt Lily's farm? What could one woman and two children do to the Union army?

Aunt Lily had tried to explain "General Sherman's Plan" to her niece—how he wanted to destroy Confederate homes. How he thought Southern soldiers would desert the army and run home when they learned of their families' troubles. But Sherman didn't know her Papa or Uncle James, Emma insisted. Those two men hadn't been fighting for over three years to lose. They would never give up.

Aunt Lily and Emma returned to the bedroom to check on Micah. He hadn't moved from his hiding place. Aunt Lily helped him into her bed, then sat on the side of it stroking his red curls. Emma wet a cloth and washed his face, which still felt warm. After a few minutes, Micah fell asleep.

Aunt Lily rose from the bed and walked to stand in front of her dressing table mirror. Her reflection winked at Emma.

"My dear, I believe those Yankees are the dumb ones."

Fat Aunt Lily removed four of the five dresses she had been wearing. Each dress had huge pockets sewn inside from which she retrieved jewelry, peach brandy, and gold coins. Last she produced a key to the locked room in the attic where she had hidden food.

That night there were sausage, potatoes, and bread for supper. Emma took a tray up to Micah, then returned to join Aunt Lily in the kitchen.

Before eating, Aunt Lily reached for Emma's hand and bowed her head.

"Dear Lord," she prayed. "Thank you for this meal. We are thankful to have food. Thank you for sparing this table so that we may gather round it. We are thankful to have each other. Thank you for sparing my farm when the Yankees have burned so many. We are thankful to have this land—which no one can take from us."

Her voice broke.

CHAPTER TWO ·

Wednesday, April 12, 1865

The next morning Old Nestor, Aunt Lily's trusted slave, returned to the farm with two horses and the buggy that he had been hiding deep in the woods.

"Nestor, after we clean up some of this mess, I want you to saddle the horses and take Emma and Micah home this afternoon," Aunt Lily said. "I promised my sister that they would return to Raleigh before this Easter weekend. She'll worry herself sick if that doesn't happen."

Emma was glad when afternoon came. They had all worked hard since breakfast, and Emma was sure Aunt Lily would continue until nightfall.

"Keep off the main roads until you get into

town," Aunt Lily instructed Old Nestor, "and I'm sure you'll be fine."

Aunt Lily put her arms around Micah. "I'm sorry your spring visit to the farm has ended this way." She placed her cheek against his forehead. "Thank goodness, no fever today."

Micah snuffled and wiped his freckled nose on his shirt sleeve.

"Try not to worry. Old Nestor will get you home safely."

"I'm not worried, Aunt Lily. I feel strong today."

Micah reached under his shirt and pulled out a forked stick.

"I can take care of those Yankees. Old Nestor made me a slingshot." Micah plucked at the piece of elastic stretched between the two ends of the stick. He pulled his ammunition from his shirt pocket— velvety green hickory nuts.

Aunt Lily managed to stop the smile that raised the corners of her mouth.

"Yes, Micah dear. I don't believe there are any Yankees who will mess with you."

She turned to her niece.

"Emma, you know that I would make this trip myself if I could leave the farm. Are you sure you can get Molly to Doc Haywood tomorrow?"

"Nothing will stop me from making the delivery to Doc," Emma assured her.

"Good girl. Here's Molly."

Emma stepped into Old Nestor's cupped hands, and he boosted her up onto the horse. Holding Molly with one hand and pulling the horse's reins with the other, Emma clicked at the horse and they began their journey home. She turned in her saddle and, waving a last goodbye, watched Aunt Lily grow smaller and smaller in the distance. She almost cried then. What if those bummers returned, and Aunt Lily all alone? But her aunt insisted the Yankees had moved on "to greener pastures."

Old Nestor and Micah rode the other horse. At first Micah sat behind Old Nestor and held onto his waist. But soon Micah turned himself around, anchoring his back against Old Nestor.

"I'm going to watch our rear for Yankees," he

said.

"You're going to fall off that horse and onto your rear," Emma scolded him.

"Nuh-uh," he said, clutching his slingshot in one hand and a hickory nut in the other. He balanced himself by sticking his legs out from the sides of the horse. On his feet were old boots, several sizes too big, that he insisted on wearing all the time.

"You look ridiculous," Emma said.

"Nuh-uh," said Micah.

They rode for two hours on forest paths. Dead leaves and pine needles muffled their movement through the thick trees and dark shade. It was four o'clock in the afternoon when they reached the streets of Raleigh.

On a normal day, there would have been horses and carriages in the streets, people entering and leaving stores, children shouting and playing outside. But today—nothing. No movement, no noise, no life. A ghost town! Had the city been abandoned?

All the doors of all the houses were closed

and all the windows were shuttered. The horses' hooves clomping on the dirt street and their own breathing were the only sounds they heard. Micah gripped Old Nestor's waist, his forgotten slingshot bobbing in his back pocket. Old Nestor kept a lookout for any signs of life, but he didn't say a word. Probably couldn't, if his mouth was as dry as Emma's.

When they reached the Graham home on Halifax Street, Old Nestor helped Micah and Emma dismount. The three of them approached the white frame house, Micah squeezing the life from his sister's hand. A knot of fear and tears began to form in Emma's throat. Where was Mother?

Suddenly the front door flew open, and Jinny, their maid, raced toward them, hands flapping the air. Her black arms scooped Micah and Emma hard against her.

"My dillies, my dillies done returned! Your Mama will be so glad to see you. She's been pacing the floor since daybreak. Nestor, you come on in and I'll fix some supper."

"Oh, Emma, Micah, thank God you're home!"

Mother cried when her children walked into the dim parlor.

"Where is everyone? What's happened?" Emma asked.

"Our soldiers left Raleigh today, dear. Everyone's locked in their houses waiting for the Yankees to arrive."

"Those demon Yankees are everywhere!"

"Emma, what do you mean?"

"They are evil, Mother." And Emma told about Aunt Lily and her farm.

"No, it can't be true," Mother said. "What will she do? She must come here at once and stay with us."

"I tried to talk her into that, Mother, but she said she couldn't leave the farm with no protection. If anyone will be safe, it is Aunt Lily. We were able to trick those Yankees."

"We might be the ones who ain't safe," Jinny said, wringing her hands. "What if those Yankees burn this very house to the ground? They done a lotta burnin' in other places."

Mother tried to reassure her. "I've been told

that Governor Vance has sent a letter to General Sherman surrendering the city. We must pray that we'll be spared."

They ate an early supper of soup and biscuits. They had to drink the soup from teacups because Mother and Jinny had buried the silver and other valuables three feet south of the well so the Yankees couldn't find them.

After supper Old Nestor insisted he needed to return to Aunt Lily.

"The Missus needs me now. I ain't afraid to rides in the dark. Prob'ly be safer."

Emma was sad to see him leave. He was a lonely-looking sight riding off on one horse, leading the other.

Late in the evening, the family and Jinny sat in the back parlor, Micah holding his loaded slingshot. Soon he began to yawn. A hickory nut rolled across the floor when sleep relaxed his hands.

"Jinny, you stay in the main house with us tonight," Mother said.

"She can sleep with me," Emma quickly offered.

Emma was bone-tired when she crawled into bed, but sleep wouldn't come. Quiet settled in around her. With wide eyes she stared into the darkness while her thoughts played leapfrog.

Would this house still be standing at this time tomorrow, or would the Yankees burn it? Would the bummers return to Aunt Lily's farm? Was Papa safe?

Emma tried to chase those thoughts away by sitting up in bed and shaking her head.

"You having trouble sleeping, Emma child?" Jinny whispered.

"Yes." Emma snuggled close against Jinny's shoulder.

"Thoughts dancing in your head?"

"Yes. I'm worried about Papa. I wish I could float up through the roof of this house and find myself hovering over Papa's camp. I'd see if he's all right. I'd bring him home with me, Jinny. And I'd make those Yankees disappear in a puff of smoke. I hate them! I hate what they did to Aunt Lily. And I'm worried about what they will do to us."

"Anyone with any sense would be scared

after what you been through with those crazy men."

"I'm not scared, just worried. I try not to get scared. Papa told me to be his brave Confederate. Those were the last words he said to me."

"I do miss that man," Jinny sighed. "And I remember clear as spring water the day your daddy walked off to war."

"That was the saddest day of my life," Emma said. Thoughts of Papa filled her mind. She closed her eyes and tried to picture every detail of Papa's face. She remembered his red hair and wide smile, but her image of him was unclear. Emma feared that one day she might forget Papa's face all together.

CHAPTER THREE

The Dream and the Turban

Emma usually didn't dream about Papa. She hadn't seen him clearly in her dreams for three years, although sometimes he was there in the shadows, and she always fought to touch him. But that night, sleeping beside Jinny, Papa came to Emma in her dream. He stood before her so real. Her dear Papa. She reached out to hug him and, just like that, he was gone.

Abruptly, she awoke and sat straight up in bed, her heart pounding and her brow damp.

"Emma . . . Emma . . . what is it? Is something wrong?" There was worry in Jinny's voice.

"I had a dream about Papa. I saw him so clear, Jinny, and then he just disappeared."

"I know, child, I know," Jinny said as she patted Emma's back. "You want to see your Papa. We all do. I always said he the finest man I know."

"Why is he the finest man, Jinny?"

Jinny's white nightcap was visible in the dark. Emma watched it move about as Jinny propped up her pillow against the bed's headboard and settled back against it.

"You know why he the finest," Jinny said.

"Tell me again. Please." Emma knew the story well, but she never tired of hearing it.

Jinny's soft voice filled the room like a lullaby.

"My old master, Mr. MacAuley, give me my freedom when he died. I done been his slave for twenty years, since I was three years old. No one would hire a free black woman until I ask your Papa. And I been with your family since before you was born."

Papa had converted one end of the barn into a nice room with a fireplace for Jinny. It smelled of wood smoke and the potpourri Mother and Jinny made from the roses they grew.

"Your mama coulda had two, three slaves workin' for her. Instead there's been only Jinny—a free woman earning her own money."

Jinny finished speaking. Quiet filled the room once again. Emma strained to hear any unusual sounds, but there were none. The Yankees weren't here yet, but everyone knew they were coming. Emma couldn't go back to sleep. And she couldn't just sit in that quiet like a little mouse waiting for a cat to pounce.

"Why do you always wear a turban, Jinny?"

"Lord, what a question! It's the middle of the night, child. Go to sleep."

"I can't, Jinny. Just talk to me."

"I wear a turban 'cause I choose to."

"How many have you got?"

"You know as well as I do."

"One black, one blue, one green," Emma said.

"Don't forget the yellow one," Jinny reminded her.

"But, Jinny, you never wear that yellow turban."

"Why, child, I wore it the day you was born

and the day Micah was born. I save it for *momentous* occasions."

"Well, I don't remember the day I was born. And I was sent to Aunt Lily's the day Micah was born. Put it on tomorrow."

"I will not."

"When then?"

"How 'bout the day your daddy comes home? Yes, ma'am, now that will be a momentous occasion. Why, I might even dance a jig. What do you say to that?"

"I say I hope Papa comes home tomorrow."

Emma knew Jinny was trying to cheer her. Next to Papa, Jinny knew Emma best. And Emma didn't have Papa anymore, at least for a while.

Talking with Jinny about Papa finally soothed her, and after a time Emma fell into a dreamless slumber.

CHAPTER FOUR

Thursday, April 13, 1865
The Morning

Emma awoke to the drumming of rain on the roof. She dressed in her red gingham dress. As she walked downstairs, she could hear the slap and pat of Jinny making biscuits in the kitchen.

Emma set the table in the dining room—four napkins and plates, no silverware, two milk glasses for Micah and her, and two cups and saucers for Mother and Jinny. Jinny had always eaten breakfast with the family so she and Mother could plan the day. She ate every meal with them now because none of them wanted to look at Papa's empty chair.

When they all gathered for breakfast, Emma buttered the brown crusty top of one of Jinny's fluffy biscuits with her finger.

"At least we'll still have butter to eat as long as we have Rosebud," Mother remarked.

"If the Yankees don't eat her," Micah said.

"That old cow would make some mighty tough beef," Jinny said as she reached for her coffee cup. After one sip she clanged the cup onto the saucer.

"What I wouldn't give for some real coffee instead of this parched corn brew!"

"Ummmmm. Dark, rich coffee with cream," Mother agreed. "But at a hundred dollars a pound, coffee's too rich for us."

After breakfast Mother waited for Micah to leave the room.

"Emma and I are going to Christ Church this morning," Mother said to Jinny.

"No, you ain't," Jinny insisted. "It's too dangerous with them Yankees a-coming."

"Now, Jinny, that church is full of wounded and sick soldiers from the battle at Bentonville. They need every available volunteer. I most certainly intend on going. Emma is old enough to help out, too, but Micah must stay here with you."

"I want to go," Emma told Jinny, whose eyes widened like a hoot owl's. Emma grabbed Molly. "I'm ready."

"Emma, really, don't you think a twelve-year-old girl is too old to be carrying a doll?" Mother asked.

"Please let me take Molly. I promise to put her in a safe place where she's out of the way."

Mother led the way to the Gothic-style stone church, walking in the pouring rain, glancing neither left nor right. Emma carried Molly and followed close behind.

Emma couldn't believe what she saw when Mother pushed open the heavy wooden door of their church. Inside the dimly lit sanctuary, the narrow wooden pews were spread with quilts and blankets, and on them lay the soldiers.

Mother pointed to a pail of water and a pile of neatly folded rags.

"Emma, take these and bathe the foreheads of those men with fevers."

"I must see Doc Haywood first," Emma said.

"Why?"

Emma ignored the question and walked away. Mother followed her. The doctor was near the front of the church.

"I have my Molly with me," Emma told him. "Aunt Lily sends her regards."

Mother stared at Emma as if she had gone crazy.

"Emma, what do you mean? You aren't making any sense."

Doc Haywood just smiled at Mother, took Molly, and pulled off her cloth head. Mother gasped. Threads dangled from the doll's stuffed body. The doctor held Molly upside down and fifteen gauze-wrapped vials plopped into his hand.

"We were getting desperate for this morphine," Doc Haywood said. "I can't thank you enough, Emma Graham."

Mother's forehead was the first one Emma had to bathe when she nearly collapsed on the floor, but Mother's weakness didn't last for long.

"Don't tell me that Lily now has you participating in her smuggling activities," Mother hissed at Emma.

"This is the first time I've ever helped her, I promise. Aunt Lily couldn't leave her farm. I had to help out. I'm just lucky that those bummers didn't get Molly."

Mother's face turned paler.

"Emma, if you ever join in such activities again, I will . . . I will . . . . Well, I don't know what I will do, but you won't like it!"

Doc Haywood handed Molly's head and body to Emma. He smiled and winked.

"Good work, you brave girl!"

There were many men with burning brows. Emma spent several hours wringing out cloths and replacing the water in the pail. Many of the soldiers were sick with dysentery. Some of them moaned. Some dictated letters to families far away.

Emma thought of Papa. Was he sick or wounded? Was there someone nursing him? Was he dead on a battlefield with no one to bury him?

"Stop it, silly," she scolded herself. "He *will* come home."

Emma stood in the gloom of the stone church. Lifting her eyes to the vaulted wooden ceiling, she offered a silent prayer from the part of her heart reserved for Papa. The part that was sore from missing him.

Emma felt a light pressure on her shoulder and turned to find Mother standing close.

"It saddens me so to see this church filled with suffering soldiers," Mother said. "It should be white with Easter lilies. Oh, for a normal life." She wrapped her arms around Emma.

Suddenly from outside they heard the far-off beating of drums and a deep rumble. The volunteers stared at one another with popping eyes.

"They've finally arrived," Mother said. She drew a shuddering breath and clutched Emma tightly.

CHAPTER FIVE

Thursday, April 13, 1865
The Afternoon

The Yankees' arrival didn't stop the suffering of the soldiers in the church. As the din of the approaching army grew louder, a volunteer summoned Mother. Emma followed her to the front of the church with a clean cloth and pail of water.

Mother sat on a low stool beside a young soldier who lay on old folded quilts. A patched grayish sheet covered him to his chin. Mother gently laid her hands on top of the soldier's. His bleary eyes slowly opened.

"Want to write my wife," he whispered through dry, cracked lips. "Ain't strong enough."

Mother patted his hands and reached for a pen and paper from another volunteer.

"It would be a privilege for me to help you," she said. "Emma, this young man could concentrate better with a cool forehead."

Emma placed a wet cloth on his furrowed brow. He relaxed and began to speak in a raspy whisper.

"Dear Caroline. I know I'm dying. I love you, and my deepest regret is that I can't be with you to say goodbye."

Mother's pen scratched slowly across the paper; she kept up easily with the soldier's halting words. She leaned closer and closer to hear him as the steady drum beats from outside grew louder.

"I'll always be with you," the soldier said. "In your favorite lilacs in the spring, in the summer sun warming your shoulders."

The soldier began to cough. Emma hurriedly wet the cloth and pressed it to his lips, squeezing slightly. A small amount of water trickled into his mouth. The coughing subsided, and he continued.

"See me in the red leaves of the maple tree outside your window, and hear my sighs when the winter winds blow. I'll be there."

Mother paused to wipe her wet cheeks. Tears welled in Emma's eyes and burned behind her nose. She suddenly felt she would faint if she didn't get away from the dying soldier.

"I need fresh water," she said, holding up her pail. Emma ran to the back of the church, dropped her pail, and leaned against the church door.

Papa! She couldn't stop thinking of Papa. Before the war, he had been there in every season of her life, in all her memories. Where was he now? Where was he?

Emma couldn't make herself return to Mother and the soldier. She needed to breathe fresh air. Slowly, she opened the heavy door and slipped outside. She would rather have Mother angry at her for leaving than cry like a baby in front of all those wounded men.

The smothering tears that had collected in her chest moved down and formed a fist of anger in her stomach as she stood outside the church in the rain. Everywhere she looked there were soldiers in blue, some walking, some on horseback.

"How dare these Yankees walk smack dab in

the middle of our streets while all we do is hide behind our window shutters?" she muttered. "I'm sick and tired of acting like a scared rabbit!"

Emma walked in the street, too—along the side, with her head down. She moved quickly, hoping the Yankees wouldn't notice her. But she refused to run.

When she reached home, Emma found Jinny hopping around the kitchen like a cricket after a rain.

"Oh, Miss Emma, Doc Haywood's girl done been here, and what she told me is terrible, just terrible. The governor and all those gov'ment men done high-tailed it outta town. Ain't nobody left over at the Capitol building 'cept Simon Battle, and I know he scared to death!"

"Calm down, Jinny. Simon was probably out of that building before Governor Vance himself."

"No, no. Simon's just a servant, but they give him the key to the building and told him to let those Yankees in when they arrived. And then those high and mighty men just up and left town. I'm sorely worried about Simon, but I'm too scared to go to

38

him."

"Well, I'm not scared. I'm sick of wondering what these Yankees are gonna do next. I'll go check on Simon."

Emma dashed out the back door.

"No, Miss Emma, don't go do that! Your mama will skin me alive. Come back here!"

This time Emma did run down Wilmington street, past Christ Church and onto the Capitol grounds. Hiding behind a giant oak tree, she watched the Capitol for several minutes. Rain washed down the windows and granite sides of the large domed building. She could see only one sentry, and he was walking slowly to the far side of the building.

Emma knew that Simon left the window of a first floor doorkeeper's office unlocked. She had seen Jinny and others stand at that window, visiting with him.

The window was already open. Making sure the sentry didn't see her, she climbed through it. The room was deep in shadow, and she had to feel her way to the door that led to the hallway. Inching the door open, she saw no one.

Emma tiptoed into the cool and hushed hallway. Her soggy clothes dripped a wet trail; her shoes squished with each step, so she took them off.

Moving quietly, Emma checked the governor's office. The door stood open. Piles of papers covered the large walnut desk. She listened but heard nothing except her own shallow breathing.

The building hulked around her.

"Carry on," Emma ordered herself.

She crept up the stone staircase to the second floor. At the far end of the hall she spied a tall man staring out a window at the city in the distance. Holding her breath, she squinted through the dim interior light. It was Simon!

Moving like an Indian brave, Emma sneaked up behind him. He jumped when she touched his sleeve.

"Miz Emma! What in the world you doin' here?" he whispered loudly, glancing over his right shoulder.

"Jinny is about to jump right out of her skin

worrying about you. Can I tell her you're all right?"

Simon turned back to stare out the window. His throat muscles worked up and down as he swallowed several times.

"I don't know," he said finally. "Yesterday I stood right here at this very window and watched an army shuffle away. Them soldiers wore rags. Some of 'em didn't have no shoes. Only one here and there wore anything gray. And now this mornin', here come another army. All dressed up in blue, ridin' horses or walkin' sprightly. It's a big change, Miz Emma, a big change."

"Are you going to stay here as the 'keeper of the Capitol' or go back to Doc Haywood's place?" Emma immediately clamped her hand over her mouth. She had heard Jinny and others jokingly call him that, saying Simon was the only one in that building with the same opinions and cool head from one day to the next.

"Think nothing of it, Miz Emma," he said. "I knows people calls me that sometimes. I don't take no offense. I don't rightly know what's to become of me. Now the whole gov'ment's gone, and I just don't know."

"Are you here by yourself?"

"No'm. One Yankee soldier done been in here. Said his name's Lieutenant Round. Helps send the signals for this army, he does. Wants to set up a signal station on top of this building since it's so tall."

"But the top of this building is—"

Sudden shouts and sounds of breaking glass interrupted Emma. She and Simon ran to the middle of the second floor, where a round opening was encircled by a high brass and cast iron railing. Peering through it down to the first floor below, they saw large pieces of glass scattered on the stone floor. They jerked their heads upward and stared at the gaping hole in the dome's glass skylight that crowned the Capitol sixty feet overhead—and at a man caught in wire netting who was poking through the hole and scrambling to get out.

"Lieutenant Round?" Emma asked, pointing upwards.

Simon grinned.

"That's the man."

CHAPTER SIX

Thursday, April 13, 1865
The Evening

Shaking his head, Simon walked to a narrow dark stairwell.

"Now, Miz Emma, you wait right here for me. Don't follow me up."

Emma wasn't happy with Simon's instructions, and she didn't have to do what he said anyway, but she stayed put. Let him go up to the roof and check on that Yankee!

Soon she could hear muffled talking and footsteps. Simon slowly descended. Gripping Simon's shoulder for support with one hand and holding blood-soaked rags around the other, Lieutenant Round hobbled down the stairs.

"Miz Emma, the lieutenant's wrist needs

lookin' after. I'm gonna ask that sentry to get him a doctor."

"Mother's just across the street at Christ Church," Emma's mouth said before her brain could control it.

Simon hurried off and left Emma all alone with an enemy soldier. Visions of the Yankee bummer Charlie flashed before her, and her breath caught in her throat.

"Hello, miss," the Yankee said. "Could you tell me where I might sit down?"

Emma motioned for him to follow and walked stiffly toward the Senate Chamber. She had taken only a few steps when she realized the lieutenant wasn't following. Turning back to look, Emma saw his knees begin to buckle. Once again without thinking, she rushed to him, took his arm, and led him slowly to one of the mahogany desks in the Senate Chamber.

He sat down with an "umph" and lowered his head to the desk. Emma stared at the thick black hair that curled over his uniform's collar. Suddenly, she was reminded of how she used to twirl her fingers in Papa's red curls when she was a little girl.

Emma opened one of the windows, removed her handkerchief from her dress pocket, and held it out in the pouring rain. Returning to the lieutenant, she placed the cool, wet cloth on the back of his neck.

"Oh," he sighed. "Thank you."

He slowly raised his head and stared up at Emma. His coal-black eyes were piercing, yet gentle, and he reminded her of one of the new puppies on Aunt Lily's farm.

Aunt Lily! Emma hurriedly backed away from the Yankee lieutenant.

"Don't be afraid." He spoke softly to her. "I can't thank you enough for your kindness."

"I'm not being kind. I'm . . . I'm . . . helping Simon."

The lieutenant held out his good hand toward Emma.

"I'm Lieutenant George Round. And you are?"

Emma retreated further.

"I know who you are. You're a Yankee soldier. You've come to take over our city. Are you going to go house to house and steal from us and pour molasses all over our parlors? Well, are you?"

Her voice had risen on every word, and she was now screaming at the lieutenant. He stared at her with his mouth open.

"You should see what your army did to my Aunt Lily's farm. It's destroyed! The only thing they didn't do was burn her house to the ground."

"Believe me, miss," the lieutenant said, "General Sherman issued orders to protect the people of Raleigh, but it is next to impossible to control those undesirables."

"We need protection from the whole Union army, if you ask me," Emma said.

More words stood ready to spew out of her mouth, but at that moment Simon ushered Mother into the room. Her eyes flashed Emma a definite message of "I'll deal with you later." She hurried to the lieutenant and began to unwrap his bloody bandage.

"I'm Elizabeth Graham, sir. Let me clean

your injury, and then we can decide if further attention is needed."

"Mrs. Graham, I'm so grateful to you," Lieutenant Round said.

Mother and the Yankee exchanged quick smiles, but his changed to a wince as she began to clean his wrist wound. The deep cut oozed dark red blood.

"Lieutenant, you need to see your army surgeon immediately. This cut needs stitching. In the meantime I'll wrap it tightly in a clean bandage."

As Mother nursed the lieutenant, Emma noticed his long sideburns and chin beard that merged to frame his face with dark hair.

"I feel so foolish, Mrs. Graham. My orders are to establish my signal station on top of this Capitol's dome. The only way I could get to the dome was to climb up a rusty lightning rod cable."

"I'm surprised your hands aren't cut to pieces," Mother said.

"I found an iron railing around the dome's top about shoulder level. I couldn't see over the railing very well; it was dark and raining. I jumped over the railing thinking there was a solid roof on the other side."

"And you found glass," Mother said.

"Glass, a wire net, and myself dangling a hundred feet over a stone floor."

"You're a lucky man, Lieutenant."

"Lucky in many ways, Mrs. Graham. Fortunate to be alive and to have a gentle nurse attend me."

This civility was too much for Emma.

"My father is a Confederate soldier who fights with General Lee," she said, standing as tall as she could.

Mother shot her a stern look.

"You haven't heard the news, miss?" the lieutenant asked.

"What news?"

"General Lee surrendered to General Ulysses Grant in Virginia last Sunday."

Mother gasped.

"I don't believe you," Emma managed to whisper as tears filled her eyes. "The South will never surrender."

"Yes, miss," the lieutenant said. "The Confederate Army of Northern Virginia surrendered at a place called Appomattox Court House. We just received the news yesterday."

"You're lying."

"Emma, enough," Mother said. "Lieutenant, my husband has been with General Lee over three years."

"He should be coming home soon, Mrs. Graham. General Lee's soldiers were issued passes and allowed to return home after the surrender."

Emma's chest and stomach hurt as if she had been punched. She ran from the Senate Chamber and down the stairs. Despite her shoeless feet and the drenching rain, she raced the two blocks home, dodging soldiers and horses.

Jinny screamed when Emma threw open the back door, slipped, and fell into a heap on the kitchen floor.

"Oh, Lord, Miz Emma, what those Yankees done to you now!" Jinny cried, dropping to the floor and pulling Emma close.

Emma tried to tell her the lieutenant's lies, but only gasping sobs erupted from her mouth. Jinny gathered Emma into her arms, carried her upstairs, removed her soaked clothes, and put her in her warm bed.

The last thing Emma saw, before Jinny quietly closed her bedroom door, was Micah, peeking around the door frame, his questioning eyes glistening with tears.

CHAPTER SEVEN

Good Friday, April 14, 1865

Emma stared into the mirror the next morning at the red rings of puffiness that circled her eyes. They ached, like sunburn.

"You're weak," she whispered, and her reflection mouthed the same insult. "Crying like a baby, believing that man's lies. Papa is standing tall and strong somewhere right now, fighting Yankees."

Emma shut her mouth and whipped around when her door opened. Micah, wearing his boots, clomped into the bedroom, stopped, and stared at his sister.

Pointing and smiling, he turned to Jinny, who stood behind him.

"Emma's eyes look like bees played ring-around-the-rosie on them. And they stung her when they all fell down."

Normally Jinny would have smiled at Micah's infantile humor, but today she shooed him from Emma's room.

"Emma, your mama wants you in the front parlor."

Jinny's hand rested lightly on Emma's shoulder as they walked down the stairs. When they entered the parlor, Mother asked Jinny to leave and close the door. Emma knew she was in trouble.

Mother sat very straight in her chair. She motioned to Emma to sit beside her. Walking slowly toward Papa's chair, Emma dreaded what was surely to come next—Mother's disappointment in her.

Drawing a deep breath through her nose and slowly breathing out, Mother stared at Emma's eyes, then closed her own and shook her head slowly.

"Emma," she said in a soft but stern voice. "Your behavior of late is unacceptable. I know you suffered a great shock at Lily's farm. I shudder to think of it. But smuggling morphine, sneaking out of the church yesterday, running off to the Capitol, calling the lieutenant a liar . . . ."

Mother's voice quavered as she recited Emma's misdeeds. She gripped the arms of the chair to calm herself.

In a normal voice, she said, "You are to remain here in this house until I give you permission to leave it."

"Yes, ma'am." Emma looked down at her lap, at her clasped hands. The question she wanted to ask Mother stuck in her throat like dry cornbread. She opened her mouth to speak but coughed instead.

Mother placed her hand on Emma's and squeezed.

"Emma, what is it?"

"Do you believe Papa has surrendered?" she asked.

"It will be a blessed thing, Emma, for Papa to hold us in his arms when he returns. You, me, and a son he hardly knows. Now go eat your breakfast and help Jinny clean the kitchen."

Emma helped Jinny with chores all morning. They didn't talk much. In the early afternoon, Mother said Emma could go with Jinny to her room. Micah raced out the back door ahead of them and disappeared.

Emma sat and stared into Jinny's fireplace. A few coals from the early morning fire still warmed the air.

"Jinny, do you think Mother still loves Papa?"

"Laws, child, what kind of a question is that? I don't know many women who loves their man half as much as your mama loves your daddy."

"Then how can she believe that Yankee's lies, Jinny? You know Papa hasn't surrendered. He never would. How can Mother believe he has?"

"I know it's hard for you to understand, but your mama ain't thinking 'bout winning or losing or surrendering. She thinking about her man and hoping he be safe and on his way home."

"Jinny, have you ever been in love?"

"I loves this family."

"Jinny, you know I don't mean that kind of love. I mean, have you ever loved a man?"

"Emma, does you dream up questions in that head of yours to addle me? Where I gonna find a man to love who's colored and free? I ain't never seen such a creature."

"So you're never going to have your own children?"

"Well, I'll be."

Jinny stared at Emma and slowly shook her head. There'd been a lot of staring and head-shaking all day.

"You befuddle me, child! You ought to know I'm too old to think about havin' my own children. Anyways, you and Micah are my dillies, and I sure don't need any more than the two of you!"

Jinny's bed giggled.

"Micah Franklin Graham," Jinny said sternly, "are you under my bed spying on your sister and me?"

Sliding on his belly and scraping the floor with the toes of his boots, Micah scooted from under

Jinny's bed.

"You're Mr. Big Ears listenin' in on talk that's private," Jinny scolded him.

"I closed my ears and didn't listen to you," Micah said.

"I'm glad to know that." Jinny smiled.

"Have you?" he asked Jinny.

"Have I what?"

"Have you ever loved a man?" Micah asked.

Jinny sighed and rolled her eyes.

"I'm sure I loved my daddy," she said.

"You had a daddy?" Micah sounded surprised.

"What you think, Mr. Big Ears, I just sprung up full growed in a hollow tree stump?"

Micah's giggles returned.

"I was just three years old when I was bought by Mr. MacAuley and taken to his place. I don't recall much before that 'cept two things."

"What two things?" Emma asked.

"One happy thing, one scary thing."

"Tell the happy one first," Micah insisted.

"I remember walking beside a lot of water—

moving water. And this soft wind blew in my face. I walked between a man and a woman, each one holding my hand. I think it musta been my mama and daddy. All I know, I was happy." A smile creased Jinny's face as she gazed up toward the ceiling.

"Now tell the scary thing," Micah said, placing his hands up beside his ears to cover them if the telling got too scary.

"I remember being so scared it still dries up my mouth to think about it. I couldn't move, my head felt like it was on fire, and then nothing, just blackness." Jinny continued to stare into the distance, but a look of horror replaced her smile.

"That's it?" asked Micah, lowering his hands.

"It don't sound like much, but, child, I don't want you to ever be as scared as that remembering is to me."

All was quiet once again in Raleigh that evening. In the back parlor, Emma stared at the smoking stand that held Papa's cold and dusty pipes. Jinny repaired Micah's slingshot by cutting a section off the elastic to shorten it, retying it around the stick, and pulling it taut. Micah counted his stockpile of hickory nuts.

"I'm down to seven nuts," he said. "I'll need more than that when the Yankees come to our house."

"They won't come here, dear," Mother reassured him.

Micah looked disappointed.

"Are you sure they won't come? They came to Aunt Lily's way out in the country."

"But we're in the city, son, and the Yankees here are not the ruffians who attacked Lily's farm. I don't want you to worry."

"Don't you worry, Mother. I only have seven nuts left, but Mrs. Blalock has a hickory tree, and she said I could help myself to as many of those nuts as I could carry."

Suddenly, a loud knocking at the front door caused all of them to jump. Micah grabbed his repaired slingshot from Jinny's hands. All followed Mother down the hall to the front door.

On the porch stood Lieutenant Round.

"Good evening, Mrs. Graham, Miss Graham. Because of the disaster at your sister's farm, I've brought a guard to protect your house. This is Private Corey Phillips."

The lieutenant stepped aside and revealed a young soldier, his yellow hair and his blue eyes reflecting the glow of the oil lamp that Mother held.

Private Phillips raised his hand in a salute to Mother, but before his fingers could touch his cap, he grabbed his cheek and yelled, "Ouch!"

Mother whipped around and there stood Micah, holding up his slingshot while he fumbled in his pocket for another hickory nut.

"Micah!" Mother shook her finger at him.

Jinny grabbed Micah and pushed him behind her.

Mother turned to the soldier.

"Oh my, oh my," she said in a shaking voice. "Whatever can I say, Private Phillips? I don't know what has come over my son."

The soldier stared at the porch. He bent down and picked up the hickory nut, which had raised a red welt on his face.

Emma held her breath as silence hovered in the air like a storm cloud.

"It's a sad state of affairs, ma'am, when you're reduced to fighting with slingshots and nuts," the soldier said. He turned to Lieutenant Round and grinned. "I don't believe this house needs any more protection, sir."

The two men began to laugh. Mother joined in, relief flooding her face. Jinny smiled as Micah peeked out from her skirt.

Lieutenant Round squatted on his heels and motioned for Micah to come to him. Micah shuffled forward, scraping his boots, his head hung low.

"May I see your weapon, son?" the lieutenant asked.

Micah held out his forked stick, the elastic drooping again.

"You're very resourceful, young man, using what's at hand to defend yourself and your family. I admire that. But you can turn that job over to Private Phillips now."

"You mean he's not a Yankee?" Micah asked.

"Well, yes, he is," the lieutenant said, "but he

has orders to protect this family at all costs. He is going to make camp here in your front yard. You can sleep at night knowing you are safe and watched over."

"You're so kind, Lieutenant," Mother said, offering her hand. He stood and took her small hand in his. She then held out her other hand to the soldier.

"And thank you, Private Phillips. I'm so sorry."

"No offense taken, Mrs. Graham. And, please, call me Corey."

Before Emma went to bed that night, she glanced out her window at Corey's white tent in front of her house. The light from his lantern flickered as she watched the shadowy outline of him climbing onto his cot. It was the first time since returning from Aunt Lily's that she had gazed out a darkened window and not feared that Charlie's dirty, sneering face would suddenly lunge at her from the other side.

Emma shook her head and climbed into bed. Her world was just too strange of late. Too strange for words. So strange that she had not spoken since the knock sounded at the Grahams' front door.

CHAPTER EIGHT

Saturday, April 15, 1865

"Look at me! Look at me!"

Shouting woke Emma the next morning. She bolted from bed. Looking out her window, she saw Micah sitting on a horse that Corey was leading around the yard. Micah bounced in the saddle, holding onto the pommel, and then swung his legs high into the air. Emma was sure that horse was wondering what species of wild animal was on its back. Then she noticed Micah's head. Perched on it was Corey's blue Yankee cap.

Emma jumped into her clothes and raced downstairs.

"Jinny, that Yankee soldier has stolen a neighbor's horse and dressed Micah up as his Union monkey!" she yelled as she skidded into the kitchen.

Jinny didn't flinch. Her hands methodically stirred the butter churn.

"Emma, it's not good to start the day screechin' and runnin'. That there horse belongs to Mister Corey, and he's been playing with your brother for over a half hour. Micah's happy to have some man attention."

"But, Jinny, he's got Micah wearing a blue cap."

"Lordy, girl, it's just a hat. I'm wearing my blue turban today. But it don't mean I'm no Yankee, and it don't mean I'm no monkey neither."

"Jinny, this is serious."

Jinny chuckled.

Emma spent the rest of the morning cleaning her room. Cleaning her room! She *never* did that unless she was upset or being punished.

After lunch, Corey knocked at the back door and asked Mother if he could take Micah with him to the Capitol. He wanted to report to Lieutenant Round. Corey asked Emma if she would like to ride on his horse, too.

"I certainly would not!" she said.

Off they went on horseback, this time with Micah sitting in front of Corey. At least Micah had put that blue cap back where it belonged—on Private Phillips's head.

Soon Mother called Emma to the kitchen.

"Jinny promised to send some fresh butter to Lieutenant Round today, but Corey has already left. I'm on my way to Christ Church. Walk with me that far, and then I will watch you cross the street to the Capitol. You can take this butter to the lieutenant."

There was no guard at the east entrance to the Capitol when Emma arrived. She let herself in—this time through the door instead of the window. She walked quietly up the staircase to the second floor Senate Chamber. The door was partially open, so she peeked inside. There sat the lieutenant in one chair, Simon in another, deep in conversation.

"Then when I's 'bout eighteen year old I was bought by Master Brooks. Moved to a rice plantation. Now that work was wet, hot and buggy, workin' them rice fields. But sometimes the Master

65

and Missus would take some of us slaves down to the ocean to help out with a picnic and settin' up tents for shade. Now that was worth it all. Bein' beside all that water, the wind just a-blowin' in your face."

The lieutenant nodded but did not interrupt the flow of Simon's words.

"Met me the prettiest girl on that plantation. Pearl and me fell in love, jumped the broom together, and the Master give us a big supper to celebrate."

"Jumped the broom?" the lieutenant asked.

"Got ourselves named husband and wife," Simon explained. "We was happy. Had ourselves a sweet daughter after a year. Pearl left the fields and went to work in the main house. She liked that 'cause she could keep an eye on the baby."

"Where are your wife and daughter now?" asked Lieutenant Round.

Simon leaned forward and rested his elbows on his knees.

"I don't usually like to talk about it," he said.

The lieutenant placed his hand on Simon's

shoulder.

"I'm sorry, Simon. I've pried too much."

"Aw, no sir, I knows you a good man. You couldn'ta known about my dark days. That's what I calls them, my dark days."

Simon stared at the floor as if in a trance. Emma had never seen anyone look so sad.

"Pearl worked in the main house several year. Then one day the Missus caught her listenin' at the keyhole of the door to Master Brooks's study. That wasn't like Pearl. And she never had a chance to tell me why she did it."

"What happened?" asked Lieutenant Round.

"Missus Brooks had a bad temper that could strike as sudden as a riled snake. All us slaves thought she was half crazy anyways, especially when the weather was boilin' hot, like it was that day. She started rantin' and ravin' and didn't give Pearl a chance to speak. I didn't see what happened, but another slave in the main house told me."

Simon stopped speaking for a few moments, cleared his throat, and took a deep breath. His next words quivered in the air, and Emma had to strain to hear them.

"'I'll teach you to spy on us!' the Missus yelled at Pearl. She grabbed up our daughter, who was dryin' dishes in the kitchen, threw her down on a table, and ordered two other slave women to hold her still. That mad woman took a knife and cut off half of our daughter's ear. 'You spy again and I'll cut off the rest of it,' she told Pearl."

The lieutenant's face had turned a sickly white.

"I'm . . . I'm sorry," he said.

"Pearl ran out of that kitchen and wasn't seen for days," Simon continued. "An old slave we called the wise woman put some poultice on my daughter's ear. Then one day they called me to the edge of the waterway, and there was Pearl a-floatin' face-down in the reeds. Done killed herself. She loved that little girl so much that I knowed she couldn't live no longer 'cause her mistake brought on all the trouble."

Simon rubbed his eyes with the heels of his large leathery palms.

"I loved Pearl and I missed her, but I was a-seethin' inside at what she done. And I couldn't look at my little girl without thinkin' about Pearl and the pain we all was in. Wouldn't talk, wouldn't listen. I don't remember much at all 'bout that time, them dark days, but when they was over, my little girl had been sold and nobody knowed where to. Then I was sold several year later and come to Doc Haywood's place."

The two men sat in silence for a long time.

Finally, Lieutenant Round said, "Maybe your bright days are just now beginning. You'll have your freedom soon, Simon."

"What's that to me?" Simon asked in a puzzled voice. "Don't knows how to be free, and I's too old to learn. Might as well give a bone to a dog ain't got no teeth."

"You'll have the right to choose what makes you happy."

"Ain't never been happy since Pearl and my girl been gone."

"Never?"

"Made up my mind to git along with

everybody and everything that come my way. I's been peaceable, not happy."

"Have you ever heard the phrase 'strength of character'?" Lieutenant Round asked.

"Naw, sir."

"It's what you have, Simon. You could easily be a bitter man, full of hate, but instead you're helpful and kind. And I admire you for it."

Simon sighed. His arms relaxed and dropped between his knees. He glanced at the lieutenant and a trace of a grin touched his face.

Emma backed down the hall and pushed herself against the wall. She noticed with surprise that tears had run down her neck and soaked the collar of her dress. The "keeper of the Capitol" had had a wife who killed herself and a little girl with half an ear? Everybody liked Simon, but who in this town knew the sad story of his life?

Emma dried her face, then knocked lightly on the door and entered the Senate Chamber. Both men stood up as she walked toward them.

"Here," she said, extending the butter to Lieutenant Round. "This is from Jinny."

Emma turned to Simon, put her arms around his waist, and hugged him. He stared at her with wide eyes.

"Miz Emma!" he said, his arms raised like he didn't know what to do with them. "Why you huggin' me?"

"Because you're almost as brave as my Papa, staying here alone in this Capitol to face these Yankees. I'll bet all of Raleigh thinks that, Simon." Emma looked up into his astonished face.

She stepped back from Simon, and he lowered his arms to his sides. Twice he opened his mouth to say something, but only a breathy "uh" came out. He looked like a hop-toad with a fly caught in his throat.

CHAPTER NINE

Sunday, April 16, 1865

Easter Sunday. Emma sat on the front porch steps and thought about what this holiday would have been if not for war. She could still remember the last happy Easter, five years ago. The Graham family had all dressed up in new spring finery and walked to Christ Church. Mother and Emma led the way, holding hands. Papa had followed close behind, carrying two-month-old Micah in his arms.

After church, Mother and Jinny had scurried about in the kitchen like the house was afire, Papa said. But the house wasn't burning, a feast was cooking. Soon the family plus Aunt Lily, Uncle James, and ten other guests sat down to a huge meal of ham, turkey, beef, and oysters, vegetables, celery stalks, and pickles, and, as always, plates heaped with Jinny's biscuits. And, oh, the desserts—stewed apples with cream, pound cake, pecan and sweet potato pies.

But not this Easter. Instead of food, this Easter brought more and more of the Union Army. Thousands of soldiers continued to stream into Raleigh like a long blue snake crawling over the hills and down the roads.

Emma propped her elbows on her knees, rested her chin in her hands, and stared at Mother's rose garden. Some of the bushes were already showing thick buds that would soon open into red, yellow, and pink flowers.

"Miss Graham," Corey said, approaching Emma. "I've been watching your sad face from my tent, and I think you need some cheering up. Perhaps you would like a ride on my horse to pass the time."

"And perhaps you would like to jump on your horse and ride out of here and take all these Yankees with you," Emma retorted.

"He's a real gentle animal. Won't bite you or anything." Corey smiled at Emma.

"Excuse me, Private, are you deaf? I don't

want to ride your old horse!" Emma said, her temper rising.

She thought for sure he would leave when she said that, but the man sat down on the step beside her.

"The truth is, Miss Graham, you remind me of my sister, Abigail. Abby, I call her, and that makes her mad because, as she wrote in her last letter, she's fourteen, and grown up, and deserves to be called by her full name."

"I agree with her," Emma said, liking to be compared to an older girl. "Do you have more brothers and sisters?"

"Four more sisters and two brothers, eight of us in all. We're known as the 'Fill-Ups.' Give our family a house, and we'll fill it up with children."

Emma smiled in spite of herself.

"I haven't been home in two years. Used to joke that the army was quiet compared to our household, but I really would like to be in the middle of all that commotion, especially on a holiday."

He looked plumb pitiful as Jinny would say.

And Emma knew all too well what it was like to miss family.

"Maybe I will have a horse ride after all," she said.

Corey lifted Emma onto the big roan's back. He grasped the reins and led the horse slowly down the streets. Emma was surprised to see so many people out walking, mingling with the occupying soldiers.

It was a perfect spring day. Sunlight danced on the new leaves of the oak and elm trees that lined the streets. But Emma's delight in the day dimmed as she observed hundreds of bluecoats everywhere she turned.

The shady square at the Capitol overflowed with off-duty soldiers. Corey tried to introduce Emma to several of the soldiers he knew, but she didn't want to know their names. She preferred to think of them all as just Yankees, so she told him she was ready to go home. As they turned to leave, someone called to Corey. It was Lieutenant Round.

"I'm glad to see you out and about this fine day," the lieutenant said to Emma.

"Is there no end to this stream of Yankees?" she asked him. "I never in my life wanted to see this many."

He smiled. "From my estimates, I guess the number to be well over seventy-five thousand."

"Whoa!" said Corey. "I had no idea the number was that large."

Emma sat in disbelief.

"Private Phillips, under your escort, I would like to invite the Graham family to visit me in the Capitol this evening to view a most unusual sight."

"We can't," Emma blurted. "We'll be busy dusting furniture tonight."

Emma's insult was wasted, because Mother insisted they all go to visit Lieutenant Round when Corey issued the invitation some time later.

"How can we ignore the kindness of Corey and the lieutenant?" Mother asked.

There was a sentry at the entrance to the Capitol when they arrived that evening. He said Lieutenant Round had instructed him to bring the Graham party to the Senate Chamber.

A fire burned in one of the fireplaces to ward off the chill of the large room. Mahogany furniture and a huge brass chandelier reflected the fire's glow.

"I'm glad you came," the lieutenant said, placing a small black book on a desk. "When I'm not at my station on the roof, I spend most of my time here with my signal book copying messages to be relayed to the troops."

"As if we care," Emma muttered.

"Can we go up to your station?" Micah asked.

"I'm afraid not. It's too dangerous to take you out on the roof. Couldn't forgive myself if you slipped and fell. But follow me up to the third floor. And be careful in the stairwell. It's very steep."

When they reached the third floor room on the west side of the Capitol, Lieutenant Round raised a window.

"Come and look," he said.

In the distance, the campfires of numerous Union troops turned the sky a glowing red. As far as they could see in every direction, the horizon seemed to be lit by rising suns. Yet the night sky above twinkled with stars and the white of the moon. It was as if the world was caught between day and night.

"It is unbelievable," Mother whispered, "that war could produce such a glorious sight."

"Yes," the lieutenant agreed. "You'll be happy to know, Mrs. Graham, that your Confederate General Joe Johnston and General Sherman plan to meet tomorrow at Durham Station to begin peace talks."

"It does make me glad," Mother said.

Emma stared at her. Had she heard correctly? Mother was happy to hear of peace and Union victory?

"I'm not so glad," Emma said. "Those campfires just make me think of one thing. We are surrounded by devils. They've burned their way through the South and now they turn our skies red!"

"Concentrate on your father returning home, Miss Graham, and how happy you'll be," said Lieutenant Round.

Emma stomped back down the stairs in a

huff. The others did not follow, so she sat down in the Senate Chamber at the desk where the lieutenant had been working. She could feel the hot flush from anger and embarrassment on her face.

How dare that Union lieutenant tell her what would make her happy! Only two things could make her happy, and those were for the South to win the blasted war and for Papa to come home.

Emma looked down at the desk and noticed the small black book, its leather worn and soft. She opened it and saw many notations and drawings. It was the lieutenant's signal code book! Without thinking about consequences, she quickly slipped the book inside the pocket of her dress. Maybe the lieutenant would not be able to send his messages, and maybe the war would not be lost.

"Emma, that's stealing," a small voice whispered. Micah stood just inside the door of the chamber.

"Where are the others?" Emma asked him.

"They're coming."

"Now you listen to me, Mr. Big Eyes. This may look like stealing, but it's not. It's really a tactic."

"A tactic?"

"Yes, a secret move against the enemy."

"Is Lieutenant Round the enemy?"

"Micah, he's a Yankee."

"Still?"

"Yes, still and always."

"But he's nice."

"Never mind that. Now promise me that you will not tell anyone about this book."

"Well . . ."

"Promise me! Cross your heart and swear it."

"I . . . uh . . . swear." Her little brother's trusting eyes gazed into Emma's, and suddenly she felt a twinge of guilt.

"Cross your arms, your legs, your eyes, too, and swear again."

As he did so, Micah lost his balance and fell to the floor.

CHAPTER TEN

Monday, April 17, 1865
Morning to Early Afternoon

Emma's eyes felt scratchy from lack of sleep as she crawled out of bed the next morning at the first sign of light. Retrieving the lieutenant's code book from under her pillow, she held it before her. Now what was she to do? She knew she had to act quickly before Micah's big mouth overtook his little brain and told her secret.

Lifting Molly from the top of the dresser, Emma pulled off the doll's head and tried to squeeze the code book inside the body. There was no way it would fit. She had to come up with a better solution to get the code book to the Confederate army. Maybe Doc Haywood could help.

The code book in her dress pocket bumped her leg as Emma slowly descended the stairs. She hurriedly ate breakfast humming to herself and gazing around the room. She felt Jinny watching her with an eagle eye.

"What you singing about this morning? Last night you was mad as a hornet when you come back from the Capitol."

"Can't a person sing around here?" Emma asked, dipping her buttered biscuit into the pool of molasses on her plate, never once looking directly into Jinny's eyes.

"What you up to, girl?" Jinny persisted, thrusting one foot forward and placing her hands on her hips.

"Nuffin'," Emma mumbled through the remaining biscuit she stuffed in her mouth. She jumped up from the table and darted through the back door—right into Mother, who placed her hands on Emma's shoulders and smiled.

"Emma, dear, I'm so pleased that you are anxious to begin your washday duties. Run upstairs and check your room and Micah's for any dirty clothes that might have hidden themselves under your beds."

Emma did crawl under her bed, not to pull out dirty clothes, but to hide a black book.

Jinny chuckled when Emma trudged back through the kitchen.

"You always did love Mondays," she said.

Emma had forgotten it was washday. It was her responsibility to keep the fire going under the washtub, and washing took all morning. Mother offered to wash some of Corey's clothes in exchange for his emptying the heavy tub. Even more clothes to wash. Emma would be lucky to make it to Doc Haywood's at all.

As Emma expected, the washing took hours and the noontime meal was late. After eating, Micah and Corey headed for the front porch swing. Mother and Jinny lingered at the table discussing the weeds in the flower garden. Emma hurried upstairs and retrieved the signal code book from under her bed.

Tiptoeing downstairs, she quietly inched her way through the back door. At last! She patted her pocket and felt the outline of the code book.

Stepping away from the house, she was about to break into a run, when she heard a commotion at the front door.

"Mrs. Graham, come quick," Corey yelled. "Hurry!"

Emma raced back through the kitchen and into the hall just as Mother reached the front door. Corey leaned against the door jamb attempting to hold up a rag doll of a woman. It was Aunt Lily!

Mother grasped one arm, Jinny the other, and they guided Aunt Lily to a chair. She fell into it. Mother knelt before Aunt Lily and grabbed her knees.

"Lily, what is it? What's happened?"

Aunt Lily rolled her head against the back of the chair. Tears seeped from under her closed eyelids.

"Missus 'Lizabeth," said a voice from just outside. Mother rose and hurried to the open front door.

"Come in, Old Nestor, please. Can you tell us what is wrong?"

Old Nestor shuffled into the front parlor. He

84

stopped when he saw Aunt Lily, sadness drooping his eyes even more than old age.

"It's M . . . M . . . Massa James."

"What about James? What is it?" Mother gripped the old slave's shoulders. Old Nestor's mouth opened and closed several times, but he didn't speak.

Mother shook him. "Tell us now."

"He's . . . he's dead."

Like a rabbit in the face of danger, Emma froze as movement swelled around her. Aunt Lily began to wail. The sound terrified Micah, and he ran with his hands over his ears and buried his head in Jinny's skirt. Mother rushed to Aunt Lily and gathered her close. Old Nestor began to sob. Corey gently led him onto the front porch.

Blood rushed to Emma's head and throbbed in her ears, muting all sound as though she had been underwater too long. Somehow she knew that this scene would live with her forever, that even when she was happiest, this day would lurk at the edge of her thoughts.

Jinny lifted Micah into her arms. He laid his

head on her shoulder and clumsily locked his legs—and boots—around her waist. Following them upstairs, Emma suddenly remembered the day Uncle James had given Micah those boots.

"A man always feels safe in a sturdy pair of boots," he had said. Emma wondered where his boots were now.

"Come in with us, Emma child," Jinny said at the door of Micah's room.

"I want to be alone, Jinny."

In the privacy of her room, Emma's chest heaved with the grief she had tried to hold in. Pictures of Uncle James flashed before her. She saw him square-dancing with a laughing Aunt Lily, digging side-by-side with Old Nestor in his garden, reading stacks of books, all kinds of books, by lamplight. And she saw him teaching a young girl to feed sugar lumps to a horse with big teeth as he gently stroked the animal's nose.

Eventually, the house became as quiet as a tomb. Emma lay on her bed with her arm across her swollen eyes until Mother appeared with an exhausted Aunt Lily and settled her in Emma's room.

Poor Aunt Lily! What could Emma do to help her? She brought cold compresses and placed them on her aunt's hot forehead as she had done just days before for the soldiers at Christ Church. The day she delivered morphine to Doc Haywood. Doc Haywood! Emma felt the outline of the book in her pocket.

"Aunt Lily?"

Emma sat beside Aunt Lily on the bed and leaned over to hug her. Lily's face was pale and her dark hair spread out in tangles over Emma's pillow.

"I'm so sorry about Uncle James," Emma said. "But, Aunt Lily, I've stolen this secret signal code book from a Yankee lieutenant." She took the book from her pocket and held it before her aunt. "I'm going to ask Doc Haywood to get it to General Johnston and help us win the war."

Emma waited for Aunt Lily to tell her what a brave, smart thing she had done. Instead Lily fixed her eyes on the ceiling.

"It's no use, Emma," she said in a tired voice.

Emma stared as Aunt Lily slowly closed her

eyes. Lines of pain and sadness creased her forehead, but soon she appeared to sleep. How much did Aunt Lily have to endure at the hands of the Yankees? The detestable invaders had to be stopped! Emma would be a brave Confederate for Aunt Lily as well as for Papa. She would deliver that code book to Doc Haywood. But, first, she had to put a Yankee in his place.

Lieutenant Round. Always wanting to talk about peace. Peace! Her Uncle James dying while that Yankee pretended the war was almost over. Telling Emma her Papa would be home soon, when she knew her Papa would never surrender.

Where was Papa?

Squatting beside her bed, Emma pushed the signal code book under it, out of sight. She looked up and found Micah watching her.

"Remember, it's a tactic," she said to him as she hurried downstairs and out the back door. She had a thing or two to shout at that Yankee!

CHAPTER ELEVEN

Monday, April 17, 1865
Afternoon to Evening

Once inside the Capitol Emma found Simon cleaning ashes from one of the Senate Chamber fireplaces.

"Where's Lieutenant Round?" she demanded. "I need to speak with him right away. Is he up in his station?"

"What's wrong, Miz Emma?" Simon said. "You seem mighty upset."

"That's because I am, Simon. Now where is he?"

"He left a while back. Said it was . . . uh . . . 'urgent.' That the word he used."

All that anger and no one to yell at. Emma slumped into the nearest chair and lay her head on a desk. Like a chill in winter, a cold sadness enveloped her and her shoulders shook.

"Miz Emma, you cold? You want that I light a fire?" Simon asked, moving closer to her.

"A fire won't help," Emma said, not raising her head.

"I knows somethin's wrong with you. What is it?" Simon gently placed his hand on Emma's shoulder.

She looked at the concern etched on his face.

"It's a dark day at our house, Simon. My Uncle James is dead." And she began to cry softly.

Simon bent over Emma and rhythmically patted her back.

"I knows all about dark days, Miz Emma. And I knows that they pass away."

"Will they be dark a long time?"

"Not too long, if'n there be other happy things."

"There's not much happy about war, Simon."

"That be the truth, Miz Emma. But there's a lot happy about families, and you got a good one. I had a good one, too, a long time ago. That's when I was my happiest."

"You had a little girl, didn't you?"

"Why, yes, I sho' did."

"What was her name?"

"We called her Dilly. Now come with me, Miz Emma, I needs to get you home."

Emma expected to find a silent house when they arrived. Instead there was a loud commotion in the front parlor—Mother, Jinny, and Corey all talking at once. Micah stood in the middle of them, glancing from one to the other.

"Emma, there you are," Mother said. "Oh, hello, Simon. Have you heard the news?" Emma knew from the frantic look on Mother's face that "the news" was not good. "A Southerner has shot President Lincoln. He's dead."

"And these Yankees are goin' to burn our city to the ground!" Jinny exclaimed, twisting her hands in her skirt.

"Oh, dear God," said Mother. "That can't be true, can it, Corey?"

Corey stood there, a helpless look on his face. "I really can't say, Mrs. Graham."

"I best be getting back," Simon left through the front door. Emma followed him out to the street.

"Thank you, Simon."

"You's welcome, Miz Emma. I'm sorry for your grief."

Emma watched Simon walk away toward the Capitol. Something above the building caught her eye.

"Mother!" Emma screamed. Mother and Corey ran outside and joined Emma in the street. "Look, Mother. There's a black border around the flag over the Capitol. They've raised the black flag. The Yankees plan to burn Raleigh!"

"Corey, Corey," Mother pleaded. "Please, for us, go straight to Lieutenant Round at the Capitol and ask him. He'll know the truth." Corey left at once.

"Let's wait inside," Mother said.

It wasn't long before Corey returned.

"General Sherman has issued orders to all troops to remain with their commands and not to retaliate against the city. The black band that has been sewn around the white station flag is in mourning for President Lincoln. Nevertheless, Lieutenant Round cautions you to remain inside tonight and shutter the house."

"Will Lieutenant Round use the signal flags to relay the order?" Emma asked.

"I'm not sure," Corey answered. "But he might use them."

Emma turned to look at Micah. His bulging eyes stared back at her. Emma's heart began to gallop. How could Sherman's order be issued to the troops if she had the signal book?

"Mother, I must go quickly to Lieutenant Round."

"You will go nowhere, young lady. We must go inside at once for safety and pray that these Union soldiers will not take out their grief and anger on us."

The hours passed slowly as they sat in the front parlor, all of them except for Aunt Lily, who remained in Emma's bedroom. For once, the rumbling of hoof beats was comforting to Emma as the Union cavalry patrolled the city streets.

Emma sat with her head against the back of

Papa's chair. Like a cat pursuing its own tail, thoughts chased themselves in circles in her head. Had the Yankee troops received Sherman's order not to attack Raleigh? Or was Lieutenant Round overturning desks and ripping through papers in a mad search for his code book? And were uninformed Yankees lighting torches and preparing to destroy Raleigh?

Sleep seemed impossible, but Emma must have dozed for a short time. When she opened her eyes, Mother and Jinny were asleep. Micah was not in the parlor. Mother must have carried him upstairs to his bed. Everyone slept except Emma. It was her chance to return the code book to Lieutenant Round.

Emma slipped quietly from the parlor and tiptoed to her bedroom. Being careful not to wake Aunt Lily, she inched toward the bed and dropped down on her hands and knees. She reached under the bed with her right hand and felt along the floor. No code book! Lying on her stomach, she scooted half her body under the bed and fanned her arms out from her sides, making a snow angel in the dust. Still, nothing. Frantically, Emma pushed further under the bed, slapping the floor with her searching hands.

The bed squeaked when Aunt Lily turned on her side. Emma froze for several minutes until she knew her aunt was still asleep.

Where was that code book? Had Aunt Lily searched for it? She had seemed so uninterested. Who else would have known . . . ? Oh, no!

Moving quickly, Emma left her room and crossed the hall to Micah's. The covers on his bed were neat and smooth; no one was, or had been, sleeping there.

Like an accomplished spy, Emma rushed from Micah's bedroom, down the stairs, and through the back door without waking anyone. If the Yankees didn't kill her, she knew her mother would. But she had to find that code book and her little brother.

CHAPTER TWELVE

Monday, April 17, 1865
The Evening

Emma inhaled deeply, trying to calm the hammering in her chest. Her eyes adjusted slowly to the darkness. No light spilled from the windows of any houses. The neighbors were shut tightly inside their prison homes.

Emma crept carefully into the night. Keeping close to the deep shadows of buildings and trees, she arrived at the corner of Capitol Square. She had seen no one so far except a guard on horseback patrolling a distant street, but there was more activity at the Capitol. Three Yankee soldiers stood at the east entrance. Two sentries moved in opposite directions around the Capitol.

Dodging from tree to tree, Emma paused behind each one to make sure she had not been seen. She was close enough to hear the conversation of the three soldiers.

"As for me, I'd just as soon burn these traitors out," one said.

"It's not like we ain't done it before," a second bluecoat agreed.

"Hold on, you two hotheads. I heard not more'n an hour ago that Sherman and Johnston are making real progress in them peace talks. We might be going home soon. And won't that be . . . ."

The soldier's voice was splintered by the frantic clanging of a bell. Emma flattened herself against the tree trunk as long fingernails of fear shot up her spine. The burning of Raleigh had begun! Where was Micah?

Peering around the tree, Emma saw that the soldiers had disappeared and the sentries were not in sight. She dashed through the open east door of the Capitol and began to climb the staircase to the second floor. Her shoes clomped loudly on the granite steps, so she jerked them off, stuffed them into her dress pockets, and ran to the Senate Chamber. Earlier the lieutenant's code book, hidden in her pocket, had bumped her leg. Where was that code book?

Two Yankees were in the chamber, their heads bent over a large map. Barely hesitating, Emma silently sneaked past the open door and up the stairs to the third floor. She remembered the steps that Lieutenant Round had pointed out as leading to the hatch to the roof. Emma climbed a short, sharply curving staircase to reach it. Turning its handle, she cautiously opened the hatch.

Emma stepped onto the flat roof of the Capitol. Below her lay Raleigh and all its citizens. Peering through leafy tree boughs, she tried to make out the shapes of buildings and the outlines of roads, but the city was covered by a shroud of night. The eerie red glow of the Yankee campfires burned around her in a far-off circle.

A sudden strong breeze lifted branches of the trees below Emma and billowed out the bottom half of her dress. The shoes in her dress pockets weighted her skirt above her knees. She tentatively inched out her toes to make sure no obstructions were in her path.

Emma walked further out onto the roof. She saw that several high and wide stone levels led upward like steps to the dome of the Capitol. She reached the first level by walking up wooden steps. But there was no easy access to the next level, and it was slightly higher than her waist.

Looking around and seeing no one, Emma grasped her skirt, pulled it tight in front, and looped it over her left arm. The shoes in the skirt pockets pushed against her ribs. Placing her hands on the stone above, she pushed with her arms and swung her right leg up onto the flat surface.

When she stood, Emma found the "step" to be about four feet wide. She glanced upward and saw two more stone levels rising above her toward the dome. They were easier to scale since they were not as tall as the first one. Unfortunately, they were also more narrow.

Emma turned around and grew dizzy as she realized she was teetering on a narrow stone step at the top of the tallest building in the city. She dropped back against the smooth copper of the rounded dome and sidestepped slowly to her left.

New sights came into her view as she inched her way around the dome. The bell's loud, sharp ringing continued, and, with her next step, a fire appeared off to the left. From her high vantage point, the fire seemed rather small. Emma leaned forward and attempted to peer through night's shadowy curtain to determine the exact location of the fire.

Suddenly, silence. The bell ceased its cry of alarm, but alarm of another sort seized Emma. She flattened herself against the dome as she heard nearby voices. Two men appeared two stone levels below her.

"Lieutenant," said a man Emma did not recognize, "can you see what's burning?"

"It seems to be a vacant warehouse, Higgins," said Lieutenant Round as he peered through a telescope. "There are no other houses or businesses in the vicinity."

Emma felt tremendous relief at his words.

"I am concerned about a disturbance off to the southwest. Higgins," he continued, pointing to his right, "what do you make of that?"

Emma looked where his finger pointed and could see many pinpoints of light bobbing about. Higgins stared through the telescope for a full minute.

"Lieutenant, I'm afraid a mob may be forming. There are a lot of soldiers carrying torches and rifles."

Foolishly, Emma leaned away from the dome and took a step forward as though those few inches could magnify the scene for her. She overstepped the edge of the stone and lost her balance. Throwing her hands outward for support, Emma clutched only air and fell headlong toward the men. She screamed when her left shin hit stone, and she began to tumble forward.

CHAPTER THIRTEEN

Monday, April 17, 1865
The Cannons and the Truth

Strong hands locked around Emma's waist, breaking her fall, and pulled her upward to safety. She sat on the stone step, grasping her injured leg and crying from pain and fear.

"What in Jesse is that!" bellowed Higgins. "The Angel of Death?"

The lieutenant released Emma's waist and, jumping down to the next stone level, moved in front of her.

"Miss, whatever are you doing up here?" he said.

Emma raised her head and stared directly into his eyes.

"Oh, no, Miss Graham, is that you? Are you injured?"

"Never mind me," Emma gulped. "What is happening with that mob?"

Higgins looked through the telescope.

"I don't believe it!" he said. "Lieutenant, take a look. What do you think?"

Lieutenant Round raised the telescope to his right eye.

"Higgins, that looks like General Logan on horseback."

"Yes, sir, I believe it does."

"He's drawn his sword."

"Yes, sir, I believe he has."

"Are those cannons?"

"Yes, sir, I believe so."

"Cannons?" Emma screamed. "Lieutenant, send a signal for him to put them away. He's going to fire cannons? I must warn my family!"

Scrambling, Emma attempted to stand, ignoring the pain that shot up her left leg. Lieutenant Round grabbed her arms and forced her to sit down.

"Miss Graham, it's not what you think. Look through the telescope."

He braced the long black tube from below as Emma peered through the eyepiece.

The faraway scene leapt close before her. What had appeared as pinpoints of light were now individual soldiers holding burning torches. Their faces were lifted toward a general who moved back and forth before them, slicing the air with his sword. Directly behind him, and pointed toward the Union soldiers, was a battery of cannons.

The general stopped in front of the battery. His head jerked from side to side and Emma could see his mouth moving. He pointed his sword first toward the cannons and then toward the soldiers. Slowly, the mob began to disperse and move back toward the Union camps.

"Why, he turned those cannons on his own men," Emma said.

"Yes, I believe he did," said Higgins.

"We all have orders from General Sherman to remain with our units and to leave Raleigh and its citizens at peace," Lieutenant Round said. "Obviously, General Logan intends to obey that order at all costs."

The lieutenant reached for his telescope, handed it to Higgins, and turned to Emma once again.

"Miss Graham, you never answered my question. What are you doing up here? Don't you realize how extremely dangerous it is?"

"Yes," Emma answered him. "But I had to see you. There are things I need to tell you. I—"

"Now's not the time to tell me. We must get you down off this roof. Higgins, lead the way. I'll follow behind Miss Graham and make sure she doesn't fall again."

"But, Lieutenant—"

"Not now, Emma!"

It was no use arguing with that Yankee. Emma had something important to tell him. Didn't he realize that? She also had some questions she needed to ask him. Emma followed Higgins down the steps from the first stone level to the roof, through the hatch, and down to the second floor.

The three of them entered the Senate Chamber, Lieutenant Round guiding Emma to one of the desks. He asked her to sit down.

"Lieutenant Round, I must tell you—"

"Someone must attend your injury, Miss Graham."

"My mother can see to it. I'm really not badly hurt. Bruised but not bleeding."

"I must get you home immediately. I'm sure your mother is worried."

"Lieutenant Round, please listen to me. Last night when we toured the Capitol with you, and I got mad at you when you told me I should be happy because Papa is coming home—"

"Yes, I remember," he said.

"Well, I did something I probably shouldn't have . . . and . . . I came to tell you the truth . . . and—"

Suddenly her words were interrupted by a commotion at the Senate Chamber door.

"Lieutenant," one of the sentries shouted as he entered the chamber. "You won't believe what we've got here." He turned toward the door as the other sentry walked through it, pulling someone behind him, someone who was struggling to get away.

"Micah!"

Micah stopped squirming and looked up.

"What is the meaning of dragging this boy in here?" Lieutenant Round asked.

"Sir, we saw him sneaking around outside. We didn't think much of it at first, but look what we found in his possession." The sentry extended his arm and opened his hand.

"It's your code book, sir. This little rascal had your signal code book. We have detained him downstairs, sir, attempting to question him, but he refuses to talk to anyone but you."

"Micah," said Lieutenant Round. "You could have waited until morning to return the book to me. I would have managed without it tonight. Most of those signals are encoded right here." The lieutenant pointed to his head.

Emma's mouth hung open as she stared at him.

"I was sure my code book must have fallen from my pocket as I accompanied you home from the Capitol. I'm so glad you kept it safe for me. Sentry, you can release the prisoner now."

"But, Lieutenant, he actually tried to attack me," the sentry said, pulling Micah's slingshot and two hickory nuts from his pocket.

"Can you blame him, Private? He's an innocent boy."

"Uh, yes, sir," said the sentry, and he and his partner left the Senate Chamber.

"Perhaps you'd better get back up to the roof, Higgins," said the lieutenant. "Keep an eye on things."

After Higgins left, Lieutenant Round turned to Micah and Emma.

"Well, now, this has turned into an even more eventful evening than I had anticipated. I must get you two home. Is there anything you would like to share with me before we leave?" He held up the code book.

Emma stared at the floor. She wanted to say something to express the relief and thankfulness that filled her at that moment, but her tongue felt thick and paralyzed.

Micah, however, seemed to have no such difficulty.

"Was that a lie you told those sentries?" he asked, looking up at the lieutenant. "Or was it a tactic?"

"Excuse me?"

"You told that sentry that you dropped your signal book at our house last night," Micah said. "But you didn't. So did you tell a lie or a tactic?"

The lieutenant looked confused.

"Emma said it was a tactic when she took your signal book last night. It wasn't stealing."

"Is that right?" asked the lieutenant, glancing at Emma.

"I promised her I wouldn't tell anyone," Micah continued.

"I see," said Lieutenant Round. He turned to face Emma.

Reluctantly looking into his questioning eyes, Emma was a mouse caught in a trap.

"We were scared," her voice squeaked. "Scared that you would need your signal book to send Sherman's order to the Yankees. The order not to burn our city."

"Are you still a Yankee, Lieutenant Round?"

109

Micah asked.

"I would say so."

"Oh. So those men who caught me aren't your enemy?"

"No. They're Yankees just like me."

"But I ain't no Yankee," Micah said. "So why did you tell a lie, I mean, a tactic for me?"

"You're my friend, Micah."

"Know what, Lieutenant? Tactics are confusing things."

After Lieutenant Round safely returned Emma and Micah to their house, he hurried away. Emma told Mother the whole truth about the lieutenant's signal code book and how he saved Micah and her from a Yankee prison.

The confession made Emma feel better, but later when she closed her eyes to sleep, all she could see was Lieutenant Round's face. And all she could hear were the words of gratitude to him that banged around inside her head, unspoken.

CHAPTER FOURTEEN

Tuesday and Wednesday,
April 18-19, 1865

Tuesday morning found Emma banished to her room, Mother's words of the night before echoing in her ears: "My disappointment in my children is so great I cannot endure even seeing their faces before noon tomorrow."

Emma sat by her bedroom window, alone, like a lump of dough with no leaven in it, exhausted and motionless. Her stomach rumbled occasionally from lack of Jinny's biscuits, but there were no rumblings of Yankee guns or horses. Raleigh had survived Lincoln's assassination.

Toward midday, Jinny slipped into Emma's room.

"Dinner is on the table. Your mama wants you to join us."

Emma was surprised to see Aunt Lily seated in the dining room, still pale but lacking the red, puffy eyes from yesterday. Aunt Lily attempted a smile when Emma hugged her before sitting at the table.

They all held hands as Mother said grace. Aunt Lily squeezed Emma's hand on the "Amen."

"I guess it's a good thing I'm currently an object of pity," Aunt Lily said to Emma. "Otherwise, your mother would have disowned me for turning you into a smuggler and a thief."

"Lily!" Mother said. "I would never do such a thing. I—"

"Don't deny my influence on Emma, Elizabeth. I must face it myself. What was I thinking when I asked this child to deliver morphine to Doc Haywood? The danger she could have faced because of me! If nothing else, I emboldened her to steal that code book from Lieutenant Round."

"Don't talk about me as if I'm not here," Emma interrupted. "I did the things I did because I'm helping the Confederacy. I'm doing what Papa is doing."

Aunt Lily dropped her hands into her lap and sat staring down at them. She swallowed hard, twice.

"Emma," she said. "Your father is no longer fighting. His army has surrendered. We must face that this war is at its end."

Emma stared at Micah who sat on the floor spinning a top, which whirled and whirled itself until it lost its momentum and wobbled to a stop.

"Aunt Lily, that is just a rumor these Yankees are spreading to make us think the war is over."

"No, Emma, I've seen them."

"Who? The bummers? Have they been back?"

"No, dear, I've seen Lee's men. For the last few days I've seen them walking down the roads, sometimes alone, sometimes in twos or threes."

"But how do you know they're Lee's men?"

"I've talked to them. They've shown me their safe passes."

"What's a safe pass?" Micah asked.

"It's a slip of paper that states that the man is a paroled prisoner of the Army of Northern Virginia and has permission to go to his home and remain there undisturbed."

"A paroled prisoner! Papa?"

Aunt Lily gently stroked the hair away from Emma's forehead.

"I've talked to these men, Emma, and do you know? They actually soothed me. They were serious and calm, but not cast down or humiliated. They are convinced that they've given this war their best—and then some."

Aunt Lily's hands fell away from Emma and retreated to her lap, where she clasped them so tightly her knuckles turned white.

"One of the soldiers was from the western mountains, but he sought out my farm before heading home. He brought me the news of James's death at Petersburg."

Raleigh waited as one waits for the next blinding lightning bolt in a thunderous storm.

People seemed to tiptoe and whisper in their homes and about in the city. Many of the Yankee soldiers were devastated by President Lincoln's death. It surprised Emma that a number of Raleigh citizens also grieved at his "untimely passing." Several local churches held memorial services, which were attended by people who were supposed to be enemies in a war.

Emma's confusion at life grew greater every day. She didn't have a lot to say, even to Jinny. She was a perfect companion to Aunt Lily, who remained quiet and withdrawn. They often sat together in the front porch swing, Aunt Lily alone with her thoughts, Emma alone with hers.

Mostly Emma thought about Papa. And more and more she thought of him not as a soldier, but as a man who was on his way home to his family. Happiness engulfed her when she imagined him filling their home once again with laughter and energy.

But occasionally a painful thought would leap unbidden into Emma's consciousness, and it was impossible to deny. If Uncle James was dead, was Papa dead, too? Was the messenger bearing news of Papa's death only footsteps away from bringing further grief to the family? Of course, this thought Emma kept entirely to herself, believing that it would remain untrue as long as it remained unspoken.

CHAPTER FIFTEEN

Thursday, April 20, 1865

The somber mood in the city shifted to one of hope and expectation. News circulated that Generals Johnston and Sherman had reached an agreement that had been sent to Washington City for the approval of the commanding officer of the entire Union army, General Ulysses S. Grant. An official truce was in effect.

That afternoon, while Aunt Lily napped, Micah climbed into the swing beside Emma.

"What's a truce?" he asked.

"When both sides agree to stop fighting."

A long silence followed, which was unusual when Micah was nearby.

"Why isn't Papa home by now?" he finally asked. And before Emma could stop him, he asked his next question. "Is he dead like Uncle

James?"

"Why did you say that, Mr. Big Mouth?" Emma scolded. "Now that you've said it, it might come true!"

Emma moved away from Micah and curled herself tightly into one corner of the swing. Clenching her fists and squeezing her eyes shut, she willed Micah's words into eternal silence.

Eventually Emma relaxed her tensed muscles and became aware that there had been no movement or noise for a long time. Turning in the swing, she was shocked to see Micah still there. He was staring at her as if in a trance, his eyes round as saucers and dripping tears.

"Micah?"

"I've killed Papa?" he whispered.

At once Emma regretted her outburst. Gathering Micah in her arms, she dried his face and twirled her finger in his red curls.

"I shouldn't have said such a silly thing. Of course, you've done nothing wrong. I'm just worried about Papa, too."

"Maybe that's Papa," Micah said, pointing to

a lone figure walking slowly down the street two blocks away.

"Afraid not. Papa is a big tall man."

Micah and Emma watched the man as he shuffled down the street. He reminded Emma of the scarecrow in Aunt Lily's garden, the way his clothes hung on his stick body.

Micah stood up.

"I'm going inside. Want to come? Emma?"

Emma continued to stare at the approaching man. Something familiar in the way he walked caused her to hold her breath. She moved like a sleepwalker down the porch steps and through the front gate and stood in the middle of the street. Her breath came in short, quick gasps.

The man walked closer and suddenly stopped. He reached up with his right hand and removed his hat. Dazzling sunbeams reflected off his red hair.

"Papa! Papa!"

The man threw his hat into the air and held his arm out for Emma as she raced toward him.

He pressed her close to his chest, squeezing tighter and tighter as though he couldn't hold her close enough.

Papa, skinny and hard, so different from the softer man who had left years before. His clothes were tattered, and his dusty shoes, lacking laces, flopped on his feet.

"Emma, my Emma," he cried, tears streaming down his face. "You've grown. I can't believe how you've grown. And who's this?"

Turning, Emma saw Micah standing close by, his back straight as an arrow as he stood at attention.

"Are you my Papa?" he asked.

"I am if you are Micah Graham."

"Yes, sir," Micah said, knocking himself in the head with a stiff-handed salute.

Papa bent down and Micah ran to him, clutching his neck like a vine encircling a fence post. Papa lifted Micah in his right arm. Emma ran to his left side and tucked her hand under his sleeve. When she did so, her fingers met with just cloth between them. She glanced down, saw no hand, and realized that Papa's sleeve was empty.

Emma dropped the coat sleeve and stepped back. Papa and Micah continued to walk toward the house. Their shouts had apparently alerted others. Some neighbors stood in their front yards and clapped as Papa passed by. Micah waved at them, and Papa nodded.

Mother stood at the front gate, arms outstretched to receive her precious man. A welcome smile creased Aunt Lily's face as her hands flutter-clapped beneath her chin. Jinny hopped from one foot to the other in her excitement. Even Corey stood close by with a big smile on his face, and he appeared to be trying his best not to cry.

Emma stood rooted in shock in the middle of the street. She had never envisioned a homecoming like this, never considered that the joy of this wonderful moment could be lessened by someone who said he was her Papa but appeared to be a one-armed scarecrow of a man.

CHAPTER SIXTEEN

Friday, April 21, 1865

Mother put Papa to bed less than an hour after he arrived. There was so much to tell him, so much to ask. But no matter how determined he was to remain awake, his eyes kept closing. Mother finally insisted that he give up and go to bed.

Emma had been secretly relieved. Her heart beat with joy knowing Papa was safe and asleep in his bedroom upstairs. But she preferred imagining the Papa she remembered, the burly redhead who gave her bear hugs and filled their house with hearty laughter.

Today theirs was a house of whispers. Although it was early afternoon, Papa still slept. Mother checked on him every hour to make sure she wasn't dreaming and that he was still breathing. She and Jinny had whispered to Corey early in the morning, and then he had disappeared. When he returned, the three barricaded themselves in the kitchen.

Jinny served the midday meal to Micah and Emma at the dining room table.

"What's happening in the kitchen?" Emma asked.

Jinny shushed Emma with a "just you wait."

Emma's instructions were to keep a close watch over her little brother and not to let him sneak up and disturb Papa.

Today of all days, Emma wanted to be alone with her thoughts. Instead she had to spend her time with a five-year-old who didn't have any idea what it meant to whisper.

Micah cupped his hands around his mouth and made his voice breathy.

"You have to lower the volume of your voice," Emma told him. "Don't talk so loud."

"That's what I'm doing."

"No, you're not. You sound like Reverend Mason when he softens his voice just to get the congregation's attention. But you can still hear him at the back of the church."

"Nuh-uh," Micah insisted loudly.

"Shhh. Don't wake Papa."

Micah cupped his mouth.

"You lied to me about Papa, Emma."

"What do you mean?"

"He's tall and skinny, not tall and big."

"He's been wounded in a war and walked over a hundred miles to return to us, Micah. What do you expect?"

"I know he's my Papa, though," Micah continued as if Emma had not spoken. "Because Mother said for sure he's the same man. But I wish he still had both arms 'cause now who's going to teach me to shoot a rifle? You need two hands to do that."

"Why, you selfish little ninny—"

"It's all right, Emma," Papa said, standing in the doorway of the parlor. He walked to his chair and sat down. He held his hand out for

Micah, who crawled up into his lap.

"Son, don't worry. When the time comes, we will have figured out a way for me to handle a rifle. I'm getting used to making necessary adjustments."

His smiling eyes looked at Emma.

"Emma, come sit by us," Papa said.

She watched Micah play with the empty sleeve of Papa's shirt. He rolled it up until the cylinder of material met the stump of Papa's arm, just above where his elbow should have been. Micah released the roll and watched the shirt sleeve quickly unfurl.

"There," he said, tucking the end of the sleeve into Papa's left trouser pocket. "That should hold it out of the way."

Papa kissed the top of Micah's head, and looked at Emma expectantly.

"I can't sit now, Papa. I must let the others know you're awake." Emma turned to walk to the kitchen.

Jinny stood in the parlor doorway watching them.

"Don't you let nobody near the kitchen, and this is as far as you can come," she told Emma. "I'll bring Mr. Graham a little something to eat on a tray in here."

What was going on? How could Mother and Jinny keep secrets from Emma and allow Corey, a Yankee, to be a part of their surprise?

In the late afternoon delicious aromas filled the house. Mother instructed all of them to put on their best finery. Of course, after years of war, their best did not look very fine. But it was a change from the worn calico dresses of every day.

Emma's blue crinoline dress was a hand-me-down from Aunt Lily that Mother had altered to fit her quite well. Jinny parted Emma's hair in the middle, pulled it smooth over her temples, and fashioned ringlets at the nape of her neck. Emma felt very elegant and grown-up.

The dining room table was set in gleaming china, crystal, and silver. Someone had been busy digging. Emma guessed that Mother was convinced the truce would last and there was no further threat to her treasures.

Mother was radiant in a rust silk gown with leg-of-mutton sleeves. Aunt Lily was conservatively dressed in dark gray, but her occasional smile was beautiful to see.

"What are you doing at a family dinner?" Emma asked Corey when he appeared.

"My daughter means to say, 'Thank you, Corey, for retrieving our tableware and for the dozens of errands you ran for us today,'" Mother interrupted with a sharp glance in Emma's direction.

"Our guest of honor is arrived," Micah trumpeted as he entered the dining room just ahead of Papa. Micah wore a red shirt with black suspenders. He had tried to part his hair on the side, but already it was springing back into place. Papa wore a brocade vest and a white ruffled shirt that hung on his slight frame, but in spite of that, he cut quite a dashing figure with his red curls cavorting as wildly as Micah's.

They all stood behind their chairs at the

table. One place remained empty.

"Where's Jinny?" Emma asked.

"Why, here she be on a *momentous* occasion," a familiar voice called. "And she sorry she be late."

Jinny swept into the room in her best black dress, and adorning her head was her bright yellow turban. Micah and Emma clapped in delight as the stage was now set for an unforgettable celebration.

"I believe I may embarrass myself by drooling," Papa said, "in a house of such tempting smells." Mother instructed all to sit as she and Jinny disappeared into the kitchen.

"Let our celebration feast begin!" she piped, entering the dining room with a large platter full of fried chicken. Jinny followed with bowls of green beans, new potatoes, cream gravy and a plate of hot biscuits.

Emma ate the best meal she'd had in months. The silence around the table told her that the others must be feeling the same tasty delight.

When everyone began to sigh and rub their stomachs, Mother cautioned them to save room for dessert. The highlight of the meal was sweet potato pie, which she cut into large servings.

Emma took ten minutes to eat her pie. With sugar being almost as scarce as coffee, she had not eaten any desserts for so long. She savored each sweet mouthful until it almost dissolved on her tongue.

"I'm saving at least one piece of pie for a special guest who will be calling in the morning," Mother said, and she would say no more.

Soon after the meal, Aunt Lily said she was tired and went to bed. Corey excused himself with a "Thank you sooooo much." Micah and Emma helped Mother and Jinny with the cleanup, and then they all joined Papa on the front porch.

Papa had dusted off and cleaned his favorite pipe. The burning tobacco smelled rich and sweet in the balmy night air. Mother sat beside him in the swing, and he put his arm around her shoulders. Emma's feet moved one step in the direction of the seat on Papa's other side, but she pulled herself up short and sat on the top porch step instead. Micah climbed onto the swing beside Papa and leaned his head against Papa's shoulder.

Jinny sat in a front porch rocker. Glancing in her direction, Emma found Jinny staring at her with an eagle eye. Emma couldn't look away from the disapproving gaze that impaled her with its fierceness.

"Emma can sleep in my room tonight," Jinny said to Mother. "Miz Lily looked mighty tired when she went up to bed. She could use a solitary night's sleep."

"Thank you, Jinny," Mother said. "How considerate."

Jinny began to walk toward the barn. Emma got up to follow her. When she was halfway down the steps, Papa called, "Good night, Emma."

"Good night, Papa." She smiled. "Good night, Mother and Micah."

Emma continued to Jinny's room. She knew she should have walked back to that swing and hugged them all. But how could Papa return the hug without feeling awkward, what with one arm around Mother and one arm on a Virginia battlefield?

The room was cool and dark. Jinny snatched an oil lamp, lit it, and placed it on the table by her bed.

"Here's a clean nightshirt you can wear," she said, tossing the garment on the far side of the bed.

"Jinny, can you help me with my dress buttons?" Emma asked, standing at the foot of the bed and turning her back to Jinny.

Emma could tell by the way Jinny jerked and pulled at the buttons that something was wrong.

"Jinny, are you angry with me?"

"Angry? Why, I'm mad as a hornet with you."

"Whatever for? I thought tonight was

wonderful, didn't you?"

"Don't shine the light on me, girl, turn it on yourself. You know ain't nobody in this town as glad to see your daddy as I am, 'ceptin' your mama, o' course. In fact, I think I'm about the onliest one in this room that's even halfway glad."

"How can you say that? I'm thrilled that Papa is home."

"You's got a mighty funny way of showing it. Don't think I ain't noticed, Emma. The way you keep your distance from your daddy. A quick peck on the cheek and you already backing up from him. Won't sit or stand close to him. What else can I think?"

"I'm . . . I'm . . . just giving Micah . . . a chance . . . a chance to get to know Papa the way I already do."

"You may fool yourself with those words, but you ain't fooling old Jinny. You ashamed of your daddy 'cause he just got one arm."

The accusation hung in the air between them. Emma stared into Jinny's seething black eyes and opened her mouth to deny what had been said, but not finding the words, she lowered her head.

"Law, girl, you should be on your knees thanking the good Lord that your daddy back at all. Would you rather that be Mr. James sitting on that front porch and your daddy in a cold grave in a strange place?" Jinny paced back and forth waving her hands all around.

"Jinny, please, listen to me. I'm worried about how other people will treat Papa. I don't want them to pity him because he's different than he was when he went away."

"I don't know one solitary person that would ever feel that way about a man done spent the last years in honorable fighting."

"But why did Papa have to lose his arm, Jinny? He lost the war. Isn't that enough? He's so different. He must be so sad. And he hasn't laughed once."

"You go on and bellyache about how this war done changed things. Your daddy is the same man what left here over three years ago—a mite skinnier, that's true, but the same man on the inside where it counts. What you don't know is the things that make your daddy special are all there. They didn't get chopped away with his arm."

Emma sat down on the bed beside the oil lamp and hid her face in her hands.

"I hate to think how you would turn away from your old Jinny if'n you ever thought I changed. I just might lose all my teeth or poke out an eye. What would happen then, Miss Emma? Look at me!"

Emma raised her head and reluctantly looked at Jinny.

"I would chop my ear from my own head if'n I coulda had a daddy in my life the way you had yours—and the way you got him again."

"I would never turn away from you, Jinny."

"Well, the way you been a-acting says different."

Jinny got into bed and turned her rigid back to Emma.

CHAPTER SEVENTEEN

Saturday, April 22, 1865

Emma slept that Friday night curled in a small tight ball in Jinny's bed.

When the door opened the following morning and Mother peaked around it, Jinny was nowhere in sight.

"So, you are awake, sleepyhead. Would you like to help me shave your father this morning?"

Emma pushed her arms into the robe Mother had brought and followed her into the house.

"There's my favorite girl," Papa said. "How about getting back to some old times?"

It had been a Sunday morning ritual at the Graham house that Mother would shave Papa and Emma would be her assistant.

"I'm sorry, sir, but this is not Sunday," Mother teased. "Maybe I shouldn't spoil you."

"You owe me for three years of missed Sundays," Papa insisted.

"Well . . . we do need to get rid of those scruffy whiskers." Mother smiled as she lovingly touched Papa's stubbly cheek.

Just as Emma would always remember hearing of Uncle James's death, she would remember as vividly this special morning. Papa sat in the kitchen. The sunlight streamed through the open window, bright and warm, and turned Papa's hair into curly fire. The cherry tree just outside the window was bursting with sweet blossoms, and their fragrance wafted in on a gentle breeze and filled the room.

Papa's gray eyes twinkled as he smiled at Emma. Even skinny and one-armed, he was still a handsome man.

Mother lathered Papa's face. With careful motions, she stroked the razor down his cheeks, up his neck, and over his chin. Emma stared at his pale skin as she gently wiped away the leftover lather with a warm cloth.

Emma remembered Jinny's words from the night before.

"The things that make your daddy special are all there."

Emma knew Papa's pale skin would tan; she knew he would gain weight eating Jinny's cooking. But would he ever be the strong man who made Emma feel so safe and happy? Would their house be filled again with Papa's booming laugh, or would it seem as empty as his sleeve? This new Papa was a stranger to Emma.

Later in the morning, Mother asked Emma to milk Rosebud because Jinny was running errands. Hoping to get back in Jinny's good graces, Emma rushed to the barn.

As she pulled rhythmically on the cow's full udder, streams of fresh milk rang on the side of the metal pail. The barn door opened, and Micah entered.

"A Yankee is in the parlor," he said.

"Corey might as well be in the parlor,"

Emma said. "He ate at our dining table last night."

"No, not Corey. Another Yankee. The special person Mother saved that piece of pie for."

"Who?"

"Guess."

"I will not."

"I heard Mother tell Papa that the Yankee was the one to thank for making last night so special."

"Micah, you're telling a big lie."

"Nuh-uh. Mother said he got us the chicken and the sugar for the pies."

"Last night would have been special if all we had to eat and drink were dirt and creek water," Emma said. "Now tell me what Yankee is in our parlor."

"I know and you don't, and you can't make me tell!" Micah yelled as he ran out of the barn.

Emma returned to the house with a full pail of milk and walked immediately to the parlor door. It was closed, but she could hear men's voices inside. She crept close to the door and listened, being careful not to slosh the milk.

"I'm very glad you've returned safely, Mr. Graham. Your family has been so kind to me since the first day I entered Raleigh."

Emma recognized Lieutenant Round's voice.

"Lieutenant, I owe you many thanks as well, especially for seeing that a guard was stationed at my home. Corey has become a friend to our family."

"I would have wanted my family protected in similar fashion if the circumstances had been reversed," Lieutenant Round replied.

"Last night I ate the first meat I've eaten in many weeks. Thank you for helping obtain the provisions."

"You must tell Mrs. Graham," the lieutenant said, "that this is the best pumpkin pie I've ever tasted."

"Actually, it's sweet potato, and therein lies all the difference," Papa told him.

"What was it like at Appomattox, sir, if I

may ask?"

"Like an unbelievable dream," answered Papa. "Every Confederate soldier was required to march to the center of the village and throw down his weapon. General Lee led the way on his horse. The Union soldiers lined the road on both sides leading into the village. We followed in single file behind General Lee—hundreds of us. We feared marching between the two lines of Union men."

"I, too, would have dreaded the humiliation," the lieutenant offered.

"But, you know," Papa continued, "it wasn't like that at all. The Union soldiers, our mortal enemies just hours before, stood silent and at attention as we marched between them. They began to salute us as we moved past. Tears fell from the eyes of many. The silence was broken only by an occasional sob and the ring of metal as we threw our rifles into the growing pile in the center of the village."

"I wish I could have witnessed what you describe, Mr. Graham."

"It was a pivotal moment for me, Lieutenant. I began to realize that these men were as weary of this infernal conflict as we were. All of us wanted to return to what was the truest and most precious in our lives—our families and our homes."

In the long silence that followed, Emma recalled another conversation she had eavesdropped upon. It had been in the Capitol when the lieutenant and Simon had discussed the importance of family. When Simon had described his dark days. When Simon had described the loss of his wife and daughter.

Snatches of past conversations began to ping from one side of Emma's brain to the other. They were all related, but how?

Lost in her thoughts, Emma leaned against the parlor door, forgetting that the latch on that door never fully caught. She heard a click and then a thud as the door sprang open and she fell like a sack of flour onto the parlor floor. Milk spilled, and the pail clattered across the room.

Emma squeezed her eyes shut, and her

face burned. She lay on the floor not knowing what to say or how to get out of there.

Slowly, Emma opened her eyes. Papa and Lieutenant Round stood over her. Their eyes bulged, and their mouths gaped open—which was a funny sight when viewed upside-down. Emma smiled.

Papa bent down, crooked his arm, and offered it to Emma. Reaching up, Emma laced her fingers over his arm and held tightly as he stood and lifted her to stand beside him.

"Milk anyone?" Emma asked.

The muscles in the lieutenant's face twitched as he fought not to smile, but he lost the battle. He snorted when his laughter escaped.

Papa's chest heaved twice before he threw back his head and began to laugh. The sound bounced off the walls and down from the ceiling. The deep, contagious laughter surged through the doorway and flowed through the house. It filled Emma's ears; it filled her head; it filled her heart. Like a church bell ringing out a celebration, the booming laugh announced to

Emma that her beloved Papa had returned.

CHAPTER EIGHTEEN

Wednesday, April 26, 1865

Like a child who has been forced to sit still for too long, Raleigh began to play. It seemed almost like a holiday as citizens and soldiers intermingled, as Union bands offered free concerts, as everyone anticipated the end of the war.

On Monday, April 24, General Ulysses Grant arrived in Raleigh and brought with him the sad news that the terms worked out by Sherman and Johnston to end the war had been rejected in Washington City.

But nothing could squelch the happiness in the Graham house. Papa grew stronger and laughed more each day.

"It's the magic in my cooking!" Jinny

insisted.

Emma spent more time with Papa, tying his shoes in the morning, lighting his pipe at night.

"My Emma done returned," Jinny whispered to her with a smile one evening as Emma helped clear the supper dishes.

Life was better than it had been in a long time, but a suspicion was growing in Emma, one that had been born outside the parlor door before she doused the room with milk. The suspicion nagged at her like the itch from a chigger bite.

On Wednesday morning Emma sat by the open window of her room enjoying the gentle breeze that billowed the curtains. She watched Jinny walk toward the front gate, her errand basket swinging on her arm. She stopped suddenly and set the basket on the ground. It had always been a habit of Jinny's to check and recheck her turban, and she did that now. The turban was as much a part of Jinny as her clear eyes and soft smile. In fact, Emma had never seen Jinny without a turban.

Emma sat in deep thought long after Jinny had walked away down the street. What was she to do? She thought she knew a secret that no one else even suspected. Actually, one person did know half of the secret, but this fact worsened Emma's predicament. The person was Lieutenant Round. Could she ask him for help?

Emma knew she had been rude and ungrateful to the lieutenant ever since he had arrived in Raleigh. She had cut him with sharp words every time he had offered his help. But by Wednesday evening the secret was more of a burden than Emma could bear alone.

Lieutenant Round welcomed Emma with a warm smile when she was announced to him in the Senate Chamber.

"Miss Graham, did you know that Generals Johnston and Sherman have been meeting again today to try to work out acceptable peace terms? Please tell your father and Corey this news for me."

"Lieutenant, I've come here to apologize to

you. The things I've said, the things I've done."

"No need for apologies, Miss Graham," Lieutenant Round said. "You seem so very upset. Is something else troubling you?"

His friendly face helped to loosen Emma's tongue, and she told him all her suspicions and the secret she had figured out over the last four days.

"But what if I'm wrong, Lieutenant? I don't want to hurt or humiliate Jinny. What should I do?"

"Miss Graham, I admire the thought you have given to this decision of whether to try and confirm your deductions. Honestly, I believe it's worth the risk. Because, if you are right, the truth will give a special freedom to people who have spent their lifetimes yearning for it."

Emma did not hesitate to accept the guidance of the lieutenant's words.

"Thank you for helping me decide. I'm sure it's the right thing to do." She smiled up into Lieutenant Round's face as she shook his hand.

Just then they heard shouts from outside.

The lieutenant tensed. "Listen," he said.

Through the open chamber window they could hear the sharp pounding of a horse's hooves as it approached at a fast clip. The lieutenant raced to the window to make out the rider's loud cries. Suddenly, he whipped around to face Emma.

"Miss Graham, just do as I say. Ask no questions. Race home and return to the Capitol grounds immediately with all the family members you can gather. Be sure to bring Corey."

Emma began running toward the stairs.

"Oh, and Miss Graham, tell them I have momentous news!"

She managed a few more steps before he yelled again.

"And watch the heavens!"

Her feet barely skimmed the ground as Emma raced home. It was dark, and lamps glowed from many windows. She slammed through the back door of her house and skidded to a stop in front of Papa.

"Lieutenant Round says we must all hurry as fast as possible to the grounds of the Capitol," she managed to say between gulps for air.

"Emma, it's late. Where have you been?" Mother demanded.

Emma pulled at Papa's arm.

"We'll save the questions for later, Elizabeth," Papa said, sensing the urgency. "Let's go with Emma now. Lily and Jinny and Micah, too?"

"Yes, Papa. And Corey. Where is he?"

"In his tent, I believe."

"I'll get Corey."

Everyone hurried out the back door as Emma dashed through the front. She yelled through the tent flap.

"Corey! Lieutenant Round needs you on the Capitol grounds right away."

"Why?"

"Don't waste time asking questions. He just said for us to come there immediately—and to watch the heavens." Emma shouted the last words over her shoulder as she ran toward the back of the house.

"What does he mean, 'watch the heavens'?" Corey asked, catching up with Emma and grabbing her arm.

"I'm not sure. Hurry! My family has already left. Catch up with them. I need to get something, and then I'll follow you."

As Corey ran toward the Capitol, Emma dashed into Jinny's room, pulled her yellow turban off a nail in the wall, and stuffed it in her pocket.

In just a few minutes they all stood in a circle on the grounds of the Capitol.

"What's happening?" Aunt Lily asked.

"It must be mighty important to pull a body out of their home into pitch-dark night," complained Jinny.

Just then they heard a pop and a whoosh.

"What was that?" Micah stared wide-eyed at Papa.

Before Papa could open his mouth to answer, a rocket exploded over the dome of the Capitol. Twinkling red rubies lit the night sky. As they dissolved into the darkness, another rocket exploded blue fire. A third rocket rained red sparkles, a fourth one blue.

"Corey, what does it mean?" Papa asked.

"Attention. It requests everyone to pay close attention."

Rocket after rocket began to explode. White, green, blue, green. The showers of color reached their zenith then began to fall and fade toward the earth. White, green. Red, red. White, green, blue. White, green.

"Oh, my God," Corey shouted, jumping up and down. "He's just spelled out 'peace.' The war must be over!"

Windows all around the city began to open. People ran into their yards. Union soldiers began to whoop for joy and shoot their guns into the air.

Several minutes passed with no further activity from atop the Capitol. Then, suddenly, more rockets began to explode and color the heavens with twinkling sparks of red, white, green, blue, and yellow.

" 'Peace on earth. Good will to men.' That's the message." Corey's voice choked with emotion.

The Graham family began to dance around and hug one another. Soon others joined in the celebration. A wave of people surged onto the Capitol grounds, laughing, sobbing, shouting their joy.

A long time passed before the Grahams left this sea of jubilation and walked to the Senate Chamber.

They barely recognized Lieutenant Round. One of the signal rockets had misfired, burning away his eyebrows, eye lashes, and whiskers, leaving him looking like a boiled lobster.

"Lieutenant," Emma said. "You must be in awful pain."

"I'm not very presentable, I know," he said, "and I'm sure it pains you to have to look at me, but I especially wanted to share this wonderful moment with the Graham family. Wait here for just a few minutes."

The lieutenant soon returned accompanied by Simon.

Emma smiled at Lieutenant Round. He nodded and winked at her. Walking over to

Jinny, Emma took her arm and led her into the glow from the fire that crackled in the fireplace. At the same time, the lieutenant did likewise to Simon.

"What's going on here?" Jinny asked.

Emma ignored her question. Looking up into Simon's confused face, she asked him, "Isn't Jinny just a dilly?"

"Why, yes'm, I guess she is."

"Jinny," Emma said. "Take off your turban."

Mother gasped.

"Emma, what are—" Papa began.

"This is a momentous occasion, Jinny, and you need to be wearing this." Emma pulled the yellow turban from her pocket.

"Why, you's right, Emma child. This is a day for my yellow turban."

Jinny reached up and unwound her blue turban. Emma placed the yellow one in her outstretched hand.

Lieutenant Round began to speak. He quickly recited the story of Simon's little girl and how she lost half her ear.

"Uh . . . sir . . . I tolds you that in confidence," Simon stuttered.

Jinny's eyes filled with tears. She dropped the yellow turban to the floor and stood, still as a statue, staring at Simon.

Emma moved to Jinny's left side, reached up and pulled Jinny's hair back from her face. The top half of Jinny's ear was missing. Turning to Simon, Emma gently took his hand and guided it to the side of Jinny's head. Simon touched what remained of her ear with trembling fingers.

"Dilly?" he whispered.

"Daddy?"

Simon and Jinny fell into each other's arms.

Mother's and Aunt Lily's hands flew to their open mouths. Corey and Lieutenant Round clasped one another's shoulders.

Micah, totally oblivious to the "momentous occasion," had picked up Jinny's turbans from the floor and was attempting to wrap them around his head. The material flopped over one eye.

"You look ridiculous," Emma said to him.

"Nuh-uh," said Micah.

Jinny, laughing and crying at once, turned toward Emma, who stood on Papa's left side with her arms encircling his waist.

"Emma child, you's the dilly," she said.

Emma couldn't help beaming like the sun. She had her Papa back, and Jinny had hers.

AUTHOR'S NOTE

Emma, the Graham family, Jinny and Corey are all fictional characters, but their customs, attitudes and actions are based on factual historical accounts and personal diaries of the Civil War period. The State Capitol of North Carolina was abandoned by the governor and other legislators before the Union troops arrived in April 1865. A black slave remained, alone, in the building when the enemy soldiers entered Raleigh. That slave's name is not historically documented; I have chosen to call him Simon Battle.

Lieutenant George C. Round was an actual signal officer in General Sherman's army. Emma's fictional encounters with him are based on Lieutenant Round's personal account of his experiences in Raleigh, North Carolina, at the end of the Civil War, April 13-26, 1865.

During his few days in Raleigh,

Lieutenant Round twice unintentionally risked his life. He crashed through the Capitol rotunda's skylight attempting to establish his signal station on its dome. He almost lost his life the second time when he delivered his peace message to the Union troops and Raleigh citizens. One of the signal rockets misfired, and when he went to check it, the rocket exploded in his face.

After the war, Lieutenant Round completed college and law school. He wrote to the governor of North Carolina requesting permission to settle in the state. On his journey south he decided instead to establish his home in Manassas, Virginia, which had been ravaged by the war. He became an important civic leader there, married, and raised his family.

In 1911, fifty years after the Battle of First Manassas, Lieutenant Round organized the "Peace Jubilee." It was the first reunion of surviving Union and Confederate soldiers since the end of the war in 1865. The blue and the gray lined up on opposite sides of the battlefield, walked to the middle of it, and shook hands.

Lieutenant Round died in November of 1918, near the end of World War I. He is buried in Arlington National Cemetery outside Washington, D.C.

In 1973, fifty-five years after his death, the city of Manassas, Virginia named Lieutenant George C. Round its "Man of the Century."

I owe a great deal to Lieutenant Round—a man I never met, a man who died thirty-four years before I was born. After sending his poignant message of peace and good will in April of 1865, he devoted the rest of his life to the reconciliation of his once-divided country and to the education of all citizens, both black and white. His "strength of character" was my inspiration, and I am indebted to him and to the heroism he embodied in trying times and in common life.